THE SQUIRE'S DAUGHTER

THE SQUIRE'S DAUGHTER

Ann Barker

Chivers Press • Thorndike Press
Bath, England Waterville, Maine USA

This Large Print edition is published by Chivers Press, England, and by Thorndike Press, USA.

Published in 2002 in the U.K. by arrangement with Robert Hale Ltd.

Published in 2002 in the U.S. by arrangement with Robert Hale Ltd.

U.K. Hardcover ISBN 0–7540–4815–2 (Chivers Large Print)
U.K. Softcover   ISBN 0–7540–4816–0 (Camden Large Print)
U.S. Softcover   ISBN 0–7862–3954–9 (General Series Edition)

The text of this Large Print edition is unabridged.
Other aspects of the book may vary from the original edition.

Set in 16 pt. New Times Roman.

Printed in Great Britain on acid-free paper.

British Library Cataloguing in Publication Data available

Library of Congress Cataloging-in-Publication Data

Barker, Ann.
      The squire's daughter / Ann Barker.
         p.   cm.
      ISBN 0–7862–3954–9 (lg. print : sc : alk. paper)
      1. Bath (England)—Fiction. 2. Large type books. I. Title.
PR6052.A647 S34 2002
823'.914—dc21   2001059111

Dedicated to Malcolm G, a great teacher,
and to Wesley House, 1999–2001

CHAPTER ONE

'Hush! He will hear you for sure! Do you want to surprise Richard or not?'

'We do; yes, we do!' were the whispered answers from the four children.

'Then be quiet—otherwise we will not hear him.' The children held their peace. Their oldest sister Felicity—more commonly known as Fliss—was bound to be right. Sure enough, from their hiding place inside the hollow box hedge that grew beside the gravel approach to the house, they could hear the unmistakable sound of a gentleman's boots scrunching on the stones. Christine, aged five, opening her mouth to speak, was silenced with great forethought by Fliss, who placed a hand over her mouth.

'When I say so,' mouthed Fliss silently. The four children nodded. The sound of scrunching boots moved nearer. It had to be Richard—no one else was expected. At last, the footsteps drew alongside their hiding place; Fliss whispered 'now', and they leaped out, screaming with delight, and threw themselves onto their prey. As they had hoped, he was taken completely unawares and their assault bore him to the ground. All at once though, their laughter turned to consternation, as they realized that the gentleman on the floor was not their brother, Lieutenant Richard Wintershill RN, on leave from his ship, but their neighbour and Papa's friend, Sir James Singleton.

'What's to do?' he asked from his prone position. 'Has there been an invasion?'

'Oh, Sir James! Oh my goodness me! I do beg your pardon!' exclaimed Fliss, horrified. 'Sarah! John! Christine! Helena! Get off Sir James at once, and ask his pardon!' They did as they were bid, curtseying and bowing as politely as their rather dishevelled state would permit. 'Now go inside and tidy yourselves up. Hurry!'

'What about Richard?' asked Sarah, perhaps the most persistently curious of all the children.

'We will find another way of surprising him,' she answered. 'Go now.' She turned to their victim, who was by now sitting up on the ground. 'Pray get up, Sir James.'

'I would have done so 'ere now, ma'am, but you are still holding on to my arm!' Fliss realized that in her hurry to organize the children, she had forgotten to let go of Sir James herself, and, blushing profusely, she now did so. He scrambled to his feet, then put out his hand politely to help her up. She pushed back the thick, dark-brown hair, which was constantly coming out of its chignon, and always seemed to be too heavy for her face, and looked anxiously up at him. He was a tall

2

man, strongly built, with hair a shade or two lighter than her own, fading to pepper and salt at his temples.

'I do beg your pardon, most sincerely,' said Fliss again. 'The thing is, that we are expecting Richard today and the younger ones wanted to surprise him. But—'

'But I got the surprise instead,' he finished for her. 'I take it that you do not have accurate news of when to expect your brother, Miss Wintershill.'

'No, except that it was to be late this morning.' She suddenly noticed that the visitor had not escaped unscathed from their attack. 'Oh Sir James, your coat!' she exclaimed. 'Allow me to . . .' and so saying, she began vigorously to brush the dust off the shoulders of his buff overcoat, standing on tiptoe because of his height. He endured this briefly, a smile of pure amusement crinkling the lines at the corners of his hazel eyes and lightening the rather sombre effect of the deep lines riven from his nose to the corners of his mouth.

'Enough,' he said at last with a laugh. 'I'm very grateful, but that will do, ma'am. I'm not one of your younger brothers, needing tidying up.'

Fliss blushed. 'No indeed! I beg your pardon! Please come inside. Do you wish to see Papa?'

'Thank you,' he replied. 'But first, since you have been kind enough to rectify my appearance, allow me to do you the same service.' So saying, he plucked a twig out of her hair and solemnly presented it to her.

She led the way inside, where Collins the butler took the visitor's coat and wide-brimmed hat.

'I will leave you now, Sir James,' said Fliss. 'Oh, and er, might I ask you not to . . .'

'Fear not, Miss Wintershill,' he replied, bowing slightly, his hand on his heart. 'Your secret is safe with me.' She curtsied in reply, then went upstairs to find the little ones.

'Fliss, was he very cross? Is he going to tell Papa?' asked a voice anxiously through the banisters. Fliss smiled up at Sarah, aged eight, her heavy dark hair, so much like Fliss's own, flopping into her eyes.

'I don't think so,' replied her sister, smiling reassuringly. 'He didn't seem angry at all—more amused, really.' Sarah disappeared to tell the others the glad tidings. To have earned a punishment on the very day when Richard was due home would have been too dreadful to be borne.

*　　　*　　　*

Once upstairs, Fliss met her sister Melissa in the corridor. Melissa was twenty, and together they took responsibility for the teaching of the younger ones. Melissa, with her shiny straight blonde hair, blue eyes, and nicely curved

4

figure, was commonly reckoned to be the beauty of the family. She had had a season in London two years ago, but had returned home having failed to attract a husband. She had not appeared to mind, but in repose, she sometimes had a look in her eyes which seemed to speak of unrealized hopes.

'Hello Lissa,' said Fliss. 'The children are just tidying themselves, so I thought I'd go and see Mama.'

'Not until you've done some tidying yourself, I hope,' replied her sister. 'Look at the state of your gown! What have you been doing?'

It was frequently the case that the immaculate Melissa had to remind her older sister about her appearance. Fliss looked down guiltily. There were dirty marks on the skirt of her high-necked bronze round gown from where she had knelt on the ground. Grinning impishly, she said, 'Wrestling with Sir James!' before darting off to the room which she and Melissa shared.

Downstairs, in the Jacobean panelled study, Arthur Wintershill Esquire was pouring his guest a glass of wine. The Wintershill family had lived in this vicinity for over 400 years. Sir James Singleton, however, had only lived in the village for ten years, having purchased Roache Hall, a neat, classical dwelling situated only a short distance away from Wintershill Court. Before that, he had lived mainly in

5

London, and besides the fact that he was a widower with one son of twenty, very little was known of him. It might be supposed that Sir James, as the newcomer to the vicinity, would often be in need of the advice of his long-established neighbour, but in general, advice seemed more frequently to be going the other way.

'I understand that your oldest son is due to arrive home today,' remarked Sir James.

'I believe so,' replied the squire. 'The children are very excited.'

'Yes, they certainly appeared to be when I met them outside,' answered the baronet, hiding a smile. 'Miss Wintershill was with them.'

'Fliss, you mean? She's a good girl. Just as well she's too old to be married now; I've no idea what we'd do without her.' Sir James thought of the romping hoyden whom he had just encountered. She had hardly seemed to be much older than her brothers and sisters at that moment. 'What of your own son?' went on Wintershill. 'Are we to see him again soon?'

'I think so,' replied Sir James. 'From his last letter, I gathered that he would soon be home.'

'He must be about twenty now,' said the squire.

'He was twenty last month.' They were silent for a few moments, the squire thinking hopefully of Melissa. There was no denying that William Singleton would be quite a catch,

6

for he was his father's only son, and there was no doubt that Sir James was well-to-do. Certainly Roache Hall had never been in a better state of repair, and the land that went with it was in excellent heart.

Eventually the squire said; 'It is always a pleasure to see you, Singleton; is there any way in which I may serve you?'

'It's more a case of how I may serve you,' replied Sir James with a smile. 'I think I may have found a tenant for Christmas Cottage.'

'You don't say so!' exclaimed the squire. 'That's very good of you. How comes this about?'

'It's not by any means certain,' warned Sir James. 'Someone of my acquaintance wants to retire to the country for a little while and is looking for a small property, without very much land.'

'Then Christmas Cottage would be ideal,' said Wintershill eagerly. 'When will you know?'

'I've told Mrs Grantham to get in touch with your legal man. I would think you'll hear quite soon, if she decides to take it.'

'I hope to God she will,' said the squire fervently.

The baronet thought for a moment, not wanting to pry. At last he said tentatively, 'Is it bad?'

'Not good,' replied the other, looking down into his wine. 'As you know, we had a poor

7

harvest, but then . . . well, never mind! We shall come about.' He smiled, but there was a hint of strain behind his eyes.

Sir James said diffidently, 'If a small loan would be of assistance . . .'

The squire waved his hand. 'No no, my dear fellow. I'm more than grateful to you for your offer, but borrowing really must be the last resort.' Soon afterwards, Sir James left the house, and was walking towards the gates at the end of the drive when he heard his name called. Turning, he saw Fliss hurrying towards him, her hair secured once more on the top of her head, her grubby bronze gown exchanged for one of dark green. It was not in the latest fashion, or even in the fashion before last, but of a shade that was very becoming to her.

'Sir James, I am so glad I caught you,' she said, a little breathlessly. Her cheeks were flushed with colour because she had been in haste. Certainly, she did not look twenty-five. 'I wanted to make sure that we had not hurt you in our roughness.'

'That's very kind of you, Miss Wintershill, but I'm really quite solidly made,' he smiled. 'I've suffered no ill-effects at all. Are you out to enjoy the fresh air now? May I accompany you?'

'Thank you, Sir James, but I have only come outside to gather some flowers for my mother.'

'How is she today?' he asked.

'Not well,' she replied. 'So I had better go

8

and see her, then get on with the household duties.' She made her curtsy, then hurried back into the house. He turned to watch her. How many household tasks fell on to her shoulders, he wondered. Thoughtfully, he walked the short distance back to Roache Hall.

When he had first moved in, she had been still at school in Marlborough. On leaving school, she had immediately become engaged to Rupert Bonning. Rupert's death the following year had caused her to bury herself in family concerns. Meanwhile James himself had inherited some property in Lincolnshire and had had to spend some time putting it to rights. He hardly knew Miss Wintershill; but that morning, he had had a glimpse of a young woman who rather intrigued him.

*   *   *

Once she had gathered the best of the blooms that she could find, Fliss made her way to her mother's bedchamber. Margaret Wintershill had presented her husband with living tokens of her affection nearly every year of their union, and the Wintershill children were a sturdy brood. She was frequently lying in, and at other times she was often ill. Fliss, at twenty-five, had thirteen brothers and sisters younger than herself, to whom she commonly stood as mother.

She entered her mother's chamber with the daffodils in her hand. Margaret Wintershill was sitting up in bed looking tired, even though it was only eleven in the morning. The birth of Fiona, just over a year ago, had been a difficult one. Fliss could just remember what it had been like when Mother was well, and able to enter into their interests. Now, at forty-five, she was expecting another child, and Fliss had grave concerns about her health.

'Fliss, my dear, how nice you look. What lovely daffodils you have gathered for me. Mason, put them in water, will you, please?' Mrs Wintershill's maid took the flowers, and went out. Fliss leaned over and kissed her mother's thin cheek, returning her smile.

'If I look nice, it's down to you, Mama, for you chose the material.'

'Did I really?' asked her mother, wrinkling her brow. 'It cannot be the stuff that we bought for you after you had become engaged to Rupert Bonning.'

'Yes, it is,' answered Fliss, her brow only clouding slightly at the memory of her fiancé who had died just before their wedding.

'It's lasted very well. It must be—five years old?'

'Seven,' replied Fliss quietly.

'So long,' murmured her mother. 'It's time you had something new.'

'And so I will—when the other girls are married,' answered Fliss robustly. 'They must

10

come first. After all, I've been on the shelf now for years.'

'I know,' sighed her mother. 'And it is all my fault that you and Melissa have missed your chances. If I had not been so wretchedly ill . . .'

'It was not your fault,' retorted Fliss. Seeing that her mother was becoming fretful, Fliss diverted her by telling her about the way in which she and the children had ambushed Sir James by mistake. She had no doubt that her mother would find the tale amusing, and she was not disappointed.

'I've no doubt that Sir James took it in good part,' said Mrs Wintershill.

'Yes, he did,' replied Fliss.

Mrs Wintershill looked speculatively at her daughter. 'I've always wondered whether he might not do for you,' she mused, much to her daughter's surprise.

'But Mama, he is Papa's friend, and years older than me,' said Fliss, puzzled.

'Yes, but . . .' began her mother, then Mason came in with the flowers, and she broke off what she was saying. Fliss was not altogether sorry, and she began to speak about Richard's arrival. Margaret Wintershill's face softened.

'How lovely it will be to see him. Have you spoken to Cook?' Assuring her mother that she would do so immediately, Fliss gave her a kiss and left. She thought again about the strange suggestion that her mother had made concerning Sir James. Of course, he had always been courteous, but he had never shown the slightest interest in her. In any case, after the pain that she had felt when she had lost Rupert, she had resolved not to consider marriage again. There came into her mind a picture of Sir James prone on the ground after they had knocked him down, and she could not help but giggle. He would hardly be romantically interested in her after that!

She made her way to the nursery to hold the baby for a short time, and talk to little Jane, aged three. There had been a time when she had thought that she would have children of her own. Now, it would never happen, and she could not help feeling an ache inside. After a few words with nurse, she went downstairs. Her father put his head out of the study.

'Fliss, would you come in here and help me? I'm in a muddle with the estate accounts, again.'

Just a minute, Papa. I must see Cook first, if we are to eat tonight,' she replied. After agreeing with Cook that as Richard was very fond of pigeon pie, that should certainly be provided, along with chicken in an oyster sauce, and some apple tart, Fliss returned to the book room.

'Fliss, thank goodness,' said her father in a relieved tone. 'My totals will not balance.'

'Let me have a look, Papa,' said Fliss, sitting down and taking up a pen. 'Perhaps I'll find that we have thousands more than you thought we had.'

'Would that that were so,' replied her father. 'However, we may be in for some good news, soon. Singleton came this morning to tell me that he may have found a tenant for Christmas Cottage for us.'

'Sir James?' exclaimed Fliss. 'That is very kind of him.'

'Yes, indeed,' answered Mr Wintershill. 'And he also offered to . . . er . . .' he cleared his throat—'er . . . that is, he was glad to help. My dear, I am sure that you will manage this much better if I am not here to interrupt!'

What had he been about to say? she wondered, after he had hurried out. It was strange how Sir James's name had come up in conversation with both her parents today. What had Sir James offered to do? Probably he had offered to help them financially in some way. That must be avoided at all costs. They had managed to scrape by so far without falling into debt; it would not do to start now. Shaking off her mood of abstraction, she turned to her task, and had soon made sense of the accounts.

It was quite a normal morning for Fliss. She had risen, dressed, helped the younger ones, and eaten her breakfast. She had gone to the village with some provisions for an indigent widow. She had played with the children, taken flowers to her mother, visited the nursery, spoken with the cook and the housekeeper, and organized her father's accounts. It was not quite twelve o'clock.

CHAPTER TWO

Richard arrived long after the children had given up looking for him. He seemed bronzed and fit, and delighted to be home. He had brought with him Lord Octavius Bonsor, also a lieutenant in the Royal Navy. Fliss consulted with Cook, and once she had established that there would be enough food to go round, welcomed the new arrival with pleasure.

The younger children joyfully descended the stairs to fling themselves upon their adored brother. Fliss allowed them to have their head for a time, contenting herself with making sure that no one got hurt in the mêlée.

'Do you have brothers and sisters, Lord Octavius?' she asked him, smiling, as she rang for tea.

'Yes indeed, ma'am,' he replied. 'But as I am the youngest of eight, I would be very surprised if they ever pounced on me in this way.'

'What a very odd appearance that would present,' she chuckled, and Lord Octavius joined in.

Mr Wintershill came in then and shook his oldest son's hand warmly. Richard topped his

14

father by a head, and whereas Mr Wintershill was inclined to plumpness, his son was slim, with broad shoulders.

'Well, my boy! This is splendid! The children have been waiting for you all day! Mama is longing to see you, but doesn't feel well enough to come downstairs tonight. Don't keep her waiting for too long.'

'I'll go up to her in a few minutes,' he answered. 'It's good to be home.' He looked around with pleasure, but Fliss thought that she could detect some other emotion at the back of his eyes. Then the moment was gone as, remembering his manners, he begged leave to present Lord Octavius to his father.

Shortly afterwards, it was time for the children to go upstairs. As Fliss ushered them out of the room, she observed Melissa exchanging a few words with Richard's friend, and she smiled to herself. Perhaps a little attention from their visitor would take her mind off her disappointment in London. He was undoubtedly handsome, with a fine, tall figure, and his jet-black hair and grey eyes were certainly striking.

It would be a blessing if he could be attracted to Melissa, decided Fliss, as she went downstairs later, her simple toilet complete. There were not so many young men around that they could afford to let one slip.

She had just set foot on the bottom step when there was a ring at the front door, and

Collins opened it to reveal Sir James Singleton, dressed for an evening engagement in a black brocade coat with matching breeches and a silver embroidered waistcoat, his hair neatly tied back with a black velvet ribbon.

'Sir James!' exclaimed Fliss, before she had thought properly. 'This is unexpected.'

'Oh,' he replied ruefully, coming in no further. 'Perhaps I had better go.'

'No no, by no means,' murmured Fliss. 'I . . .'

'Your father invited me to dine,' he said apologetically. 'Something tells me that he forgot to say so.'

'You are right, I'm afraid,' she answered. It was her turn to look rueful. 'But you must not think that we keep such a niggardly table that one extra will put us out! Please, Sir James, come through and join the family.' She ushered him into the drawing-room, then withdrew quietly, in order to make sure that the table was laid for one extra, and that Cook was informed that dinner would have to stretch to yet another guest! She went back upstairs to warn Melissa and Barbara to serve themselves with very small portions.

'Oh dear,' sighed Barbara. 'And I was particularly hungry tonight. Bother Sir James!'

'Never mind! We can always fill up with bread and butter later,' said Melissa.

Fliss smiled, then said, 'I will be down

16

shortly. I'll just go to the nursery to say goodnight to the children.' She was not down as quickly as she had hoped, however. Jane had some bread and jam, and in her eagerness to greet her sister, managed to get some of the sticky stuff on her gown, which meant that Fliss had to hurry and change. By the time she arrived downstairs, she was ten minutes late for dinner.

'Good heavens, Fliss!' exclaimed her father impatiently. 'What have you been doing all this time?' Fliss murmured a word of apology to the company in general. She could see that Sir James was looking annoyed, and wondered whether he was such a stickler for punctuality as her father.

Almost immediately afterwards, the party trooped into the dining-room. Fliss took her mother's place at the foot, with Lord Octavius on her right, and Richard on her left.

'Have you seen any members of your own family recently?' she asked him.

'Yes, I was up at Brigham last week— visiting my parents.'

'And were any of your brothers and sisters there?'

'Priestly, my oldest brother, lives there with his wife and children. My four sisters are all married and live away, and my brother Septimus is a soldier. And then there's Nick.' Something about the way in which he said this last name made Fliss slightly curious.

'Nick?'

Lord Octavius grinned. 'Nick is the second oldest of the family. He's the black sheep; but I have to confess that he's my favourite brother—for all that he's sixteen years older than I am.'

'I notice that some of you are named after numbers,' she ventured.

He laughed out loud then. 'Only two of us, mercifully,' he replied. 'I think that my parents ran out of ideas after six!'

'How glad I am that my parents did not use a similar scheme,' answered Fliss, 'for there were fifteen of us altogether!'

To Fliss's relief everyone seemed to have enough of everything. She and Barbara and Melissa ate sparingly; and she noticed that Sir James did as well. Richard and his friend had healthy appetites, and ate hugely of everything provided, and there was very little left at the end. After dinner, Fliss rose and led Melissa and Barbara to the drawing-room. Barbara sat down at the piano to play with her usual panache, but after a few very inaccurate bars of a piece by Clementi, she turned to face her sisters and said, 'Which of us does he favour, do you think?'

'Oh hush, Babs,' implored Fliss, looking anxiously at the closed door.

'Well one of us ought to make a push for him,' answered her shameless sister. 'After all, single men don't grow on every bush. William

Singleton ought to be mine, by rights, but there's no telling when he will be home again.'

'You are being a little previous,' remarked Melissa. 'How do we know that Lord Octavius is not already married?'

'He doesn't look married,' answered Barbara. 'He would do for you very well, Lissa. In fact, he would even do for Fliss. He must be about Richard's age, so he would only be two years younger than her.'

'He can't marry us all,' said Melissa. 'He may well not want to marry any of us.'

'He certainly will not want to marry anyone who throws herself at his head,' said Fliss firmly. 'We have only just met him, for goodness' sake! Let us maintain some decorum.'

'But let's not allow him to slip through our fingers,' responded Barbara decisively.

The gentlemen did not linger over their port, and very shortly afterwards, Richard wandered in, to be followed almost immediately by the others. Fliss rang for tea, and when the tray arrived, she poured out for everyone. Sir James was the last to take his cup.

'I waited until last, just in case,' he said softly, his amused tone taking the sting out of his words. 'If there is none left in the pot, I'll just pretend.' Fliss was about to respond indignantly when she remembered the small helpings that he had taken at the table, and she thought of the size of his frame. Her indignant flush changed to one of mortification. Too proud to apologize for her family's poverty, she recalled an earlier offence that she had committed against him.

'Sir James, pray allow me to apologize for my rudeness earlier,' she said, looking up at him with anxious eyes. 'Indeed, I did not mean to seem unwelcoming. I am afraid that my excitement at Richard's arrival made me a little flustered, and I did not greet you as I should.'

'That is not at all surprising, so busy as I know you have been,' he returned.

'Indeed I have, but I cannot tell how you should know it,' she answered a little defensively.

'My dear Miss Wintershill, to struggle into one evening outfit is enough for most of us. I have to say, however, that I think on balance that the apricot became you better.' She had to smile then.

'I went to the nursery and one of the children soiled my gown,' she admitted. 'But now you remind me of something else for which I need to apologize, for I could see how annoyed you were at my lateness.'

'I was a little irritated, but not at your lateness,' he replied somewhat abrasively. 'I hope that at my age I can manage to wait an extra five minutes for my dinner, and cannot understand why anyone else should not be able to do so! But tell me, are the young gentlemen staying for long, or is this just a brief visit?'

'Richard is staying for a few days,' she answered. 'I do not know what plans Lord Octavius has.' Suddenly remembering the bold nature of Barbara's speculation, she coloured a little.

'I hope you will all enjoy the time you spend together,' said Sir James in rather more formal tones, before joining Mr Wintershill by the fireplace. Fliss poured tea for herself, then stood up to go and join the others. Richard and his handsome friend were talking and laughing with Melissa and Barbara. Both the girls looked animated and cheerful. For a moment, she suddenly felt old and superfluous.

CHAPTER THREE

During the days that followed, Lord Octavius proved to be a most amenable guest, and to be equally pleased in any company. Whether playing ball with the younger ones, talking to Mr Wintershill, or walking with Melissa and Barbara, he appeared to be well satisfied with his lot. If he favoured either of the two of them, it was probably Melissa. Fliss found it hard to assess Melissa's feelings, for there was a vein of privacy in Melissa which meant that it was impossible to find out anything about her that she did not want known. Whatever might have been her feelings, however, Fliss was very pleased to see that her sister conducted herself with perfect decorum, neither putting herself forward unbecomingly, or losing all her conversation through shyness. She was very ready to encourage him to talk about his family, and although he was not close to all his brothers and sisters, he needed very little prompting to do so.

Fliss commented about this to her sister and Melissa simply replied, 'I think other people's families are always interesting, don't you?'

For her part, Fliss could not help noticing that Richard, once the first excitement of his arrival was over, seemed preoccupied and anxious. She had caught a hint of this mood on the evening of his arrival; now, it seemed more prevalent. Three days after his arrival, when dinner was over and whilst Melissa was playing the piano, with Lord Octavius turning the pages, Fliss asked him what was wrong.

'Nothing,' he replied. 'Why should anything be?' But his tone lacked conviction.

'Very well then,' said Fliss briskly. 'I can see that there is something the matter, but obviously you aren't prepared to tell me what it is. I shall just have to ask Lord Octavius if he knows what it might be.'

'Don't be absurd. You wouldn't do such a

thing,' answered her brother, but there was a hint of uncertainty in his voice.

'Just try me,' said Fliss, making as if to stand.

'All right then, there is something,' conceded Richard in tones that were more desperate than his sister liked, 'but I can't tell you now. Meet me tomorrow; by old Redpath, after breakfast.'

The following day, they met as arranged, next to a statue in a sunken garden in one of the more unfrequented areas around the house. The statue was of a Roman deity; but years ago, Fliss and Richard had decided that it looked far more like Nathaniel Redpath, the solicitor who dealt with their family affairs. The name had stuck, and the spot had often been a meeting place for the older ones. Fliss arrived first, a shawl around her shoulders to protect her from the chill of the early spring morning. Richard soon joined her. Now that she knew something was wrong, it seemed to her that the trouble in his face was there for all to see.

'Come and sit here,' she told him, gesturing to the stone bench. 'Tell me all about it, for I can see how disturbed you are.' He sat down, gave a deep sigh, then bowed his head, and buried it in his hands.

'I'm ruined, Fliss,' he said at last.

'Ruined, Richard?' she asked him, unable to grasp his meaning. 'I don't understand. Do you mean that you owe money?'

'What does one usually mean?' he asked, looking at her with despair in his eyes. 'Yes, I owe money; how I'm ever going to repay it is anyone's guess.'

'How much?' ventured Fliss.

'Nearly eight hundred pounds,' he answered after a pause.

'Eight hundred pounds!' she exclaimed. 'Oh Richard, how could you?'

'You don't need to reproach me,' he replied, half defiant, half contrite. 'As if I haven't told myself a hundred times already!'

'Well how came it about?' asked Fliss, judging that to scold him further would simply drive him away before she had heard the whole story.

'I'll tell you everything. A few months ago, there was a review at Portsmouth and Octavius's sister, Lady Susan Tryon, came with her daughter. Lady Susan is ten years older than Octavius, and her daughter Alice is just eighteen. Oh Fliss, you never saw a prettier girl in all your life!'

Fliss smiled. 'Go on,' she said.

'We didn't have much opportunity to talk then, but later we all met at an inn for dinner, and I managed some conversation with her. You know sometimes you meet someone and you feel as if you've known them for years? Well, it was just like that for me, and I think that it was the same for her too.

'Tavy could see that I was taken with her, and he rather thought that she liked me as well; but I knew that it would be no use. Alice has very little money. Apparently before he died, her father indulged in some unwise speculation. None of the family has any, and the ancestral home—Brigham—is mortgaged up to the hilt. Her mother wants her to make a wealthy marriage in order to revive the family fortunes. They simply can't afford for her to marry someone without means. I made up my mind to forget her.' He got up, walked away a few paces, stood in silence for a short time, then came back and sat down on the bench again. 'When Tavy arranged to go to London last week, I thought I'd go with him and see whether the delights of the town would divert me. I hadn't realized that her family would be in town so early, and when I saw her, I knew that she was the only one for me. I just had to find a way of making some money.'

'Oh Richard!' sighed Fliss, suspecting what method he had chosen to try to enrich himself.

'Yes, I know, I know,' he answered impatiently. 'Only the biggest fool on earth thinks that he can make a fortune by gambling. Well that just about proves how foolish I am, doesn't it?' He paused again, then went on quietly, looking down at his hands which he held clasped between his knees. 'I went with Tavy to one of the London gaming hells. I'd got some money with me, as I'd just been paid.' He looked up at her then. 'At first, I won quite a large sum, and I thought, this is easy! I'll soon have enough! Fool that I was! They let you win at first, you see, so that you'll stay. And then when you start to lose, they hope you'll say to yourself, I've won once; my luck is sure to turn. I was so caught up with the excitement of the game that I barely noticed when I was starting to get into debt. My losses were up almost to eight hundred pounds before I realized it. That was when I stopped.'

'Well, thank goodness for that,' said Fliss fervently. 'To whom do you owe this money?'

'Oh, a man of the town. I told him that I would return home for funds. But what I am to do, I don't know. I cannot tell Papa. The family finances are at full stretch as it is.'

'Would it not be possible for you to apply to Lord Octavius for a loan?' she enquired tentatively. Richard laughed derisively.

'Tavy has nearly as little money as I have,' he replied. 'Lissa and Barbara might as well save themselves the trouble of trying to attract him. He needs to marry money as much as Alice does.' He paused, then said, 'What am I to do, Fliss?'

She looked at him, her beloved brother who seemed at that moment to be far more than two years younger than herself. It was odd that whereas the night before, he had been refusing to tell her his troubles, today, not only had he poured out the whole story, but he was also

26

looking to her to find a solution.

'I think I may be able to find the money for you,' she said at last. 'I need to go on one or two errands, but I am almost sure that it can be managed.' The relief on his face was unmistakable.

'Fliss, you're wonderful,' he exclaimed, hugging her.

'Save your raptures until I'm successful,' she warned him.

A little more than an hour later, she was in the market town of Marlborough having driven herself there in the shabby old family gig. Soon, she was being ushered in to see the family solicitor, another Mr Redpath, but fortunately for her composure, in appearance quite unlike the statue in Mr Wintershill's garden.

'Yes, Miss Wintershill, how may I serve you?' he asked her.

'Mr Redpath,' she began, trying not to sound nervous. 'I believe that there is a sum of money in my name which becomes mine to dispose of in the event of my marriage, or on my twenty-fifth birthday.'

'That is so, Miss Wintershill,' replied Mr Redpath, after he had shuffled some of his papers around and peered at them with his spectacles. 'Whichever is the sooner. The sum I believe'—he shuffled around still more, until Fliss felt that she might scream at him—'is five hundred pounds.' Fliss nodded. It was what she had expected.

'How soon would it be possible for me to take possession of that sum of money?' she asked him.

'Am I to understand that congratulations are in order?' he replied, smiling at her in an arch way that made her long to slap him for no reason that she could think of immediately.

'Only if you wish to congratulate me on having attained my twenty-fifth birthday, and as that took place three months ago, you would be rather late,' she said a little tartly. 'It is simply that I have a use for that amount of money, and would like to obtain it as soon as possible.' Mr Redpath looked rather doubtful.

'Perhaps it might be advisable for Mr Wintershill to be involved with this,' he murmured. Anxiety for Richard's predicament made Fliss take a rather more forceful tone than was usually her wont.

'Mr Redpath, is that money mine, or is it not?'

Mr Redpath only just stopped himself from taking a step backwards. 'Well, naturally, it is yours, Miss Wintershill, but—'

'Then kindly have it sent for immediately. There is no need for my father to know anything of this matter.' She pulled on her gloves, then, glancing at his anxious face, she added in a softer tone, 'I am not considering anything criminal, I promise you.'

'Very well, Miss Wintershill,' he said with a

sigh. Then, briefly stepping over the invisible line between solicitor and client, he added, 'Please be careful!'

Five hundred pounds. Well that was the majority of it. She paused for a moment or two in the doorway, then resolutely made her way to Brumby's, the jeweller's shop. She had never been in there to purchase anything. On the other hand, she had certainly never been in there to sell, either. She had only one piece of jewellery from her grandmother, a diamond pendant of delicate design. She had always thought of it as being valuable; but she had no idea how great or little the value might be. She was very fond of it; but she told herself that Richard's safety and honour must come before diamond pendants.

A short time later, with £300 in her reticule, no pendant and a heavy heart, she was on the point of leaving the shop when Sir James came in. This was a surprising occurrence, for she had never encountered him in Marlborough before, but because of the transaction in which she had just taken part, she was unable to summon up any interest in his appearance. She bade him a subdued 'good morning'— feeling, if she was honest, not far from tears— and was about to go when the baronet said cheerfully, 'Miss Wintershill! This is a happy chance! You may be the very person to help me in my errand.'

'Your errand?' she murmured, wishing only

to leave.

'Why yes! It so happens that I need to purchase a little item of jewellery for a lady, and I wondered whether you might give me the benefit of your advice?' She looked at him blankly, scarcely taking in what he was saying. He went on, 'Your choice of er . . . adornments is always so modest and understated, that I thought . . .'

Suddenly, Fliss could not bear any more. To be commended for her good taste and discretion when the only reason for it was that she had so little was bad enough, but now, without her grandmother's pendant, she would have even less, and without the £500, she would never have a husband to buy her such little tokens as Sir James was planning to purchase today. At once, it seemed as if courtesy and discretion had entirely deserted her and all she was left with was raw pain and indignation.

'Understated? Modest?' she said sarcastically. 'How convenient for me!' Then she looked up at his face, saw the surprise in his expression, and realized how rude she had been. She flushed with mortification, stammered, 'Sir James, I . . .' Then, lost for words, she murmured, 'Excuse me,' and hurried out of the shop and down the street, almost running for fear that he might be following her to ask for some explanation. She collected the gig as quickly as she could, and forced herself to concentrate entirely on the road, so as to avoid thinking about anything more painful.

As she arrived back at the house, Richard hurried towards her, an anxious look in his eyes. Fumbling with the strings of her reticule, she pulled out the £300.

'There!' she said. 'There is part of the money. I will have the rest in a few days.' He put out his hand tentatively, as if hardly daring to touch it.

'Fliss, are you sure?' he asked. 'I mean . . . how did you get it?'

'What do you think I did? Hold up the stage? Look, just take it and keep it safe.'

'But Fliss . . .'

She nearly threw it at him then. 'Take it, I said,' she cried, indignation keeping the wobble out of her voice. 'But don't ask me any more questions, and never, never ask me for money again.' She ran up to her room, from which Melissa was thankfully absent, and sat cradling the empty pendant case whilst the tears rolled down her cheeks. 'Oh, for goodness sake, pull yourself together,' she told herself at last. 'It's only a thing after all.' But it had been hers—and sometimes, it seemed as if she had very little on which no one else had some claim.

* * *

31

That night at dinner, Mr Wintershill was in excellent spirits. Not only was Mama downstairs—looking somewhat pale, it was true, but otherwise well—but he had some good news to impart.

'We definitely have a tenant for Christmas Cottage,' he said, beaming. 'A Mrs Grantham from London is to take it. I heard from Draycott today. She is a widow and an acquaintance of Sir James Singleton. It was he who told her about the cottage.'

'Then we are very much obliged to him,' said Mrs Wintershill. Fliss looked down at her plate. She was remembering how rude she had been to Sir James that morning. Her conduct seemed doubly ungracious now that she had learned of this, his latest kindness to her family.

After dinner, the gentlemen did not linger over their port and brandy for very long. When they returned, Fliss noticed that Richard seemed to be in much more buoyant spirits than last night, and her heart lifted. Her sacrifice had been worthwhile.

As Richard was approaching to speak to his mother, Mrs Wintershill turned to Fliss and said, 'Fliss, why are you not wearing Grandmama's pendant instead of those trumpery beads?' The comment was so unexpected that for a moment she felt short of breath, and she could feel the colour rising in her cheeks.

'The catch was a little faulty,' she murmured. 'I did not want to risk losing it.' Fortunately, Mama's attention was diverted by Richard's presence, and beyond saying something about the need to have it repaired, she said no more about it. Presently, Barbara started to play the piano, and Mrs Wintershill stood up to go to the instrument.

As soon as she was out of earshot, Richard said to his sister; 'You sold Grandmama's pendant for me, didn't you?' She could not deny it.

'You needed the money,' she said simply.

'I never intended that you should do such a thing,' he said, mortified. 'I am reproved indeed.'

'Please, Richard, it's done,' she murmured wearily. 'Leave it alone.'

'I'll go to the jeweller's first thing in the morning,' he declared. 'I shall ask him to keep it on one side, and I will send him every scrap of pay that I have spare until it is redeemed!' Fliss smiled at him. His honest determination to recover the necklace warmed her heart, even while she was certain that it would be some time before she would have it in her hands again. He was off the following morning, just as he had promised, but he returned with a downcast face.

'Apparently, the pendant has already been bought,' he said.

'So quickly,' exclaimed Fliss in dismay.

'Yes. And when I pressed the assistant as to who had bought it, he told me that Sir James had done so.'

'He came into the shop as I was going out,' Fliss replied. 'He must have bought it straight away.' Sir James had said that he wanted to buy something for an acquaintance. Obviously, he had decided that her necklace was the very thing.

'There was something else,' said Richard. 'Apparently, the assistant made a mistake in the amount that was paid to you.'

'Oh no!' cried Fliss, her heart sinking into her well-worn boots. 'They want some of it back.'

'No; on the contrary, there should have been more. I have it here.' They counted it carefully.

'Richard, there is another four hundred pounds here,' said Fliss, awe-struck. 'Surely Grandmama's pendant cannot have been worth so much!'

'Do you know what I think?' said Richard. 'Sir James has spent a lot of time in London, hasn't he? Some of these society men know a prodigious amount about precious stones, you know. It wouldn't surprise me if Sir James knew more about such things than Mr Brumby. I'll wager it was at his insistence that a larger sum was paid.'

'If only I might be sure that it was not done out of charity,' sighed Fliss anxiously.

34

'Charity? Nonsense! Why should it be so? Sir James is as good a neighbour as any you'd find; but he gives his help in more discreet ways—like finding a tenant for Christmas Cottage, for example.'

'Yes, that was good of him,' reflected Fliss. 'But to return to your debt; there is now less than a hundred pounds to find. I can—'

'No, Fliss,' interrupted Richard, straightening. 'You're not selling another thing, or sacrificing another penny for me. I'll find the rest, and one day, I'll buy you another pendant, I swear it.'

Fliss smiled and hugged him. Later that day, she wrote a note to Mr Redpath telling him that she would only be needing one hundred out of the five after all. Richard might think that he could find the remainder, but it would not do any harm to be prepared. It gave her a comforting feeling that all her dowry was not gone. Somehow though, she could not imagine any gentleman wanting to marry her, unless he had a fancy for taking on the rest of the family as well.

CHAPTER FOUR

A few days later, Richard and Lord Octavius both left. Although Octavius had been a cheerful, even at times flirtatious companion, neither Barbara nor Melissa had succeeded in attaching him. Barbara certainly felt that they had been cheated, and was inclined to blame Melissa.

'You should have made more of a push to get him,' she insisted. 'Instead of which you simply monopolized him, but failed to bring him to the point!'

'Babs, please don't be so vulgar,' said Fliss. Barbara flushed.

'Well I'll beg pardon for that, but if I'd had all Melissa's chances, I would not have let him escape.'

'Babs!' This time it was Melissa who protested, her face flushed.

'I think you should go to your room,' added Fliss severely.

'All right, I'll go,' said Barbara. But she added, unrepentantly, as she went, 'Sometimes, I think I'm the only one who is prepared to make a push to achieve something for our family!'

True to his word, Richard had managed to scrape together the eighty pounds left of his debt. By a lucky chance, he found some money in the pocket of an old coat, and a small loan from Octavius made up the sum. All the family bade him an affectionate farewell, but his biggest hug was reserved for Fliss.

'You're the best sister in the world! What would I do without you?' he said, before mounting his horse and riding off down the drive with a cheery wave.

After he had left, she went to the garden to pick some flowers before setting off for St Barnabas churchyard. It was here that her late fiancé was buried. Rupert had been the only child of the Reverend and Mrs Elias Bonning. It had always been Rupert's desire to enter the church and, after he was ordained, he had been appointed curate in a neighbouring parish. He and Fliss had become engaged on her eighteenth birthday, when he was twenty-three. One year later, after visiting a sick family, he was taken ill with scarlet fever and, despite his healthy constitution, he had died.

Fliss, surrounded by a large and affectionate family, had had many people to comfort her. Mr and Mrs Bonning were devastated, and Fliss found that even in the midst of her own grief, she was needed to offer consolation to Rupert's bereaved parents.

She walked through the churchyard and paused for a few moments by Rupert's grave. There were fresh flowers there already, so Fliss walked on to the rectory with her flowers still in her hand. Vera Bonning hurried forward to greet her visitor.

'Oh, are those flowers for me? How lovely they are!' she exclaimed, as Fliss handed over the tulips that she had brought.

'Well, they are either for you or for Rupert, and he already has some.' They had never stopped mentioning Rupert in their conversations, even when it was painful to do so.

'Yes, I took some this morning,' replied the rector's wife, biting her lip. 'He would have been thirty today.'

'I know.' The two women clasped hands briefly, then Mrs Bonning said, 'I think we'll have a cup of tea.' Fliss often thought with great regret that she had never had the chance to call this gentle, kindly woman her mother-in-law as they had both once anticipated so hopefully.

There was never any shortage of conversation. Today, Fliss told the rector's wife about the visit of Richard and Lord Octavius, and something of the interest that Melissa, and particularly Barbara, had taken in their brother's handsome friend.

'But it all came to nothing in the end,' concluded Fliss. 'And now they are gone.'

'But there is another arrival in the village, I am told,' said Mrs Bonning. 'I understand that the new tenant for Christmas Cottage has taken up residence. Elias happened to be passing, and they exchanged a few words. I must call as soon as she has had a chance to settle in.'

'No doubt we will meet her during the next few days—perhaps at church on Sunday,' answered Fliss.

She was to meet Mrs Grantham sooner than expected. She walked back through the churchyard, stopping briefly by Rupert's headstone to tidy the flowers which had become a little disarranged by the wind. As she rose to her feet once more, she turned and saw Sir James standing a short distance away with a stylishly dressed lady whom she did not recognize leaning on his arm.

'Miss Wintershill,' said Sir James when they met. 'This is an unexpected pleasure. Will you allow me to introduce you to Mrs Grantham, who has taken Christmas Cottage?' The two ladies acknowledged one another politely. Inexperienced as she was in fashionable ways, Fliss could tell immediately that Mrs Grantham was dressed in the first stare. The olive green of her walking dress was very becoming to one with that shade of auburn hair, and Fliss would have been prepared to wager that her gloves were undarned, her boots unpatched, and that her bonnet had only been purchased recently.

'Miss Wintershill, I am very pleased to meet you,' said Mrs Grantham, in well-modulated tones and with a charming smile. 'James has just taken me to meet your family. It is so refreshing to find children with high spirits, but good manners as well.'

'From this, Miss Wintershill, you will infer that they didn't jump out upon Amanda as they did upon me,' put in Sir James with a smile.

'Oh good heavens! Is that customary? Do I

have it to look forward to?' asked Mrs Grantham in tones of comical dismay.

'Do not allow Sir James to alarm you, ma'am,' smiled Fliss. 'The children jumped on him by mistake. They thought that he was our brother home on leave. Richard is a lieutenant in the navy.'

'We were about to take a look around the church,' said Sir James. 'I don't suppose that you would care to accompany us?' Fliss looked at Mrs Grantham, not wanting to intrude, but could only see in her face an expression of polite interest, so she agreed.

Fliss had always been fond of the old church. It was here that she and Rupert would have been married and, after his death, she had frequently come here to sit, away from the noise and bustle that always seemed to be going on at home. Mrs Grantham appeared to be genuinely interested, and asked Fliss a number of questions about the history of the church, all of which Fliss answered to the best of her ability.

'You are clearly an expert, Miss Wintershill,' said Mrs Grantham as they left the church.

'I'm not really,' protested Fliss gently, before Sir James could say anything. 'I just love the old church. All the children were christened here, Mama and Papa were married here, and I did think to have married here myself . . .' She broke off.

'Miss Wintershill's fiancé was a clergyman,'

put in Sir James. 'He died six years ago.'

'I am very sorry to hear it,' said Mrs Grantham sympathetically. 'Was it his grave that you were tending when we saw you outside the church?'

'Yes. His father is the rector here.' They had now passed through the lych gate, and as Christmas Cottage was very close to the manor house, they naturally started to walk back together. Mrs Grantham took Sir James's left arm and, as Fliss was walking on the other side of him, he offered her his right. It was the first time that she could recall taking a gentleman's arm since Rupert's death.

'I'm afraid I cannot ask you in,' said Mrs Grantham apologetically when they reached Christmas Cottage, 'as I am still at sixes and sevens. But I hope to welcome you to drink tea with me Miss Wintershill, as soon as I have myself properly organized.' They parted in good humour, and Fliss felt that she had gained an agreeable neighbour. After that, it would have been strange had Sir James not escorted her home. Once again, he offered her his arm and she took it, but somehow it seemed far more intimate than it had when the three of them had been walking together.

'Is Mrs Grantham a widow?' asked Fliss, after they had resumed their journey.

'Yes, she is,' replied Sir James. 'Her husband was an acquaintance of mine. He died in a riding accident several years ago.'

41

'How dreadful for her!' replied Fliss with immediate sympathy.

'It was a terrible shock. I remember hearing about it.'

'Has she been living in London ever since?'

'Yes.' He paused briefly, then went on, 'I do not want to betray confidences, but I can tell you that she has not been very happy recently. Her bright manner is in part assumed, and I know that she would be very glad of friendship at this time.'

'I will gladly do what I can,' replied Fliss. At once she remembered how she had repaid his own friendship in the jeweller's shop by speaking to him immoderately. Quickly, she began to speak before she lost the courage to do so. 'Sir James, I am so very sorry for the way I behaved towards you in Brumby's the other day. I cannot explain, I—'

'My dear Miss Wintershill, you need say no more,' he answered, smiling down at her. 'We all have moments when our own company is all we want, and there is nothing for it but to rush off.' Fliss murmured thanks for his forbearance and, as they had now reached the bottom of the drive, he touched his hat to her and they parted company. Fliss started to walk up the drive, but she had not taken many steps before something made her stop and look round. Sir James was striding off towards Roache Hall, his coat swinging about him as he walked.

CHAPTER FIVE

It was not long before Fliss visited Mrs Grantham in order to take tea. She had made no plans to do so; she was on her way back from the village when her new neighbour came out of Christmas Cottage into the garden and attracted her attention.

'Miss Wintershill, are you in a hurry? Can you spare half an hour?' Fliss thought of the duties that awaited her at home. A quiet half-hour would certainly be very welcome. After only a brief hesitation, she opened the gate and walked down the garden path.

Christmas Cottage was let fully furnished, but Mrs Grantham had brought a few pieces of her own with her, and the presence of the little writing desk in the window, the matching vases on the mantel shelf and the spinet in the corner all seemed to indicate that the inhabitant had made the house entirely her own.

'Do come in and sit down,' said Mrs Grantham. 'You will see that I have been very busy, and have just about got myself straight down here.'

'It looks lovely,' said Fliss looking round.

'I can assure you that chaos still reigns upstairs,' replied her hostess confidingly, as she rang the bell. 'Tea for myself and Miss

Wintershill if you please, Grace,' she said, as soon as a middle-aged maid appeared. When the maid had gone, Mrs Grantham confided, 'Grace has been with me for years. Sometimes I think that she knows me better than I know myself. She will certainly never allow me to do anything that she thinks might be bad for me.'

'Nurse is rather like that,' replied Fliss. 'I don't think that she really believes that any of us has grown up.' At that moment, Grace brought in the tray. Mrs Grantham poured the tea, and it proved to be delicious, a fact on which Fliss felt herself bound to comment.

'I brought it with me from London,' explained Mrs Grantham. Then, after a brief pause, she went on, 'Do you get to London very often, Miss Wintershill?'

Fliss shook her head. 'I have never been at all,' she said simply.

'But how comes this about?' asked her hostess with such obviously genuine interest that her words were robbed of impertinence. 'I am sure that I was told by someone that your sister had had a season there.'

'Yes, that is true,' agreed Fliss. 'And if you have seen my sister, then I am sure that you will agree with me that such a lovely girl should not miss her chance in London!'

'Certainly I agree, but forgive me, Miss Wintershill, that does not answer my question.'

Fliss sighed. 'I became engaged when I was eighteen. Taking me to London would have been an unnecessary expense. You must not think that I repined,' she went on quickly. 'I went to Bath and was quite content with that.'

'Have you been to Bath much?' asked Mrs Grantham, as she poured them both another cup of tea. 'I should have thought that it is not a very long journey from here.'

'It isn't very far,' agreed Fliss. 'But I have not been there for several years. I've led a very narrow, uninteresting life, I'm afraid.'

'You must give me leave to tell you that I doubt that,' replied Mrs Grantham. 'Judging by what I have seen of your brothers and sisters, I think that your life has been anything but uninteresting.' There came into Fliss's mind the thought that Richard's financial excesses had made her life rather too interesting for comfort. But, shaking off the memory of what his foolishness had cost her, Fliss called to mind one or two of the children's exploits, and told them to her hostess, who rewarded her by laughing heartily.

'They certainly are lively,' she commented. 'But now I recall that the first time we met, you said something about the children ambushing James, and I have been longing to hear the whole story ever since.'

'There's very little more to say, ma'am,' replied Fliss, but she obliged by telling her new neighbour the story in detail, which made Mrs Grantham laugh once more.

'I hoped that coming to the country would do me good,' she said at last, 'And it has done so already. I cannot remember when I have laughed so much! Poor James!' she went on. 'I do trust the set of his coat was not spoiled! He has always been rather particular about his clothes.'

At that moment, there was a knock at the door and very soon the object of their present conversation was admitted to Mrs Grantham's little sitting-room. Looking at him with her hostess's comments still ringing in her ears, Fliss realized that although his clothes were of a colour and cut entirely appropriate to a country situation, yet he wore them without a wrinkle and with great style.

'May I come and drink tea with you?' he asked, sitting down and laying his hat and cane on the floor.

'I suppose I must give you some since you are here,' replied Mrs Grantham, with the ease of long acquaintance. She rang the bell in order to send for another cup and a fresh pot of tea. 'I must tell you, however, that Miss Wintershill and I very much resent the curtailing of our conversation.'

'Indeed? I suppose you were talking of things that I'm not supposed to know about,' he said.

'As a matter of fact, we were talking about you, James, were we not? Miss Wintershill was telling me something about you that would bring a blush to your cheek—were you not so full of effrontery.' The blush came to Fliss's cheek, and not Sir James's. She was not used to this kind of rallying conversation, particularly not with her father's friend, and did not know how to correct the impression that her hostess had given without making matters worse.

Sir James, however, seemed to be not at all discomposed, and merely said, 'If Miss Wintershill told you anything about me that reflects badly on my character, then I will venture to say that the truth is not in her!'

'Now how can that possibly be?' exclaimed Mrs Grantham. 'You know perfectly well that a gentleman should never contradict a lady!'

'Mrs Grantham pleases to jest,' ventured Fliss at last. 'I was only telling her the story about how we mistook you for Richard the other week, Sir James.'

'You did indeed,' he agreed. 'I still have the bruises to prove it.'

Grace came in with the tea and another cup, and Mrs Grantham poured for them all.

'By the way, James, I have heard something from Miss Wintershill that has surprised me greatly: apparently, she has not been to London. Is that not shocking?'

'I am not at all sure of that,' said he. 'Many people have gone to London who would have done much better to have stayed at home.' Fliss, unaccountably feeling that he had defended her, gave him a grateful smile, and for a moment thought that she saw him wink at her!

'Yes, but listen,' persisted Mrs Grantham, who had been adjusting the teaset and had thus not seen the wink. 'She has never been at all, James, and what is more, she has hardly been to Bath, either. What is to be done?'

'Why, nothing at present,' he returned. 'And certainly, whatever we may do must not constitute interference in Miss Wintershill's affairs.' He paused, then went on, 'Have you heard from your brother, Miss Wintershill? Is he to return to his ship soon?'

This closed the discussion of London and Bath, and Fliss could not help feeling relieved. Deep down inside, however, she was conscious of a stirring of something that was rather like discontent. She had always known that visits to such places were impossible, because of the expense, and because she was needed at home. There had been a time when she had very much longed to go to London. Only by exercising the strongest discipline had she managed to stop herself from giving voice to such desires. She had thought that by now, she would have stopped wanting to go. It was rather disturbing to discover that the old yearnings were still there, not very far from the surface.

After half an hour, Fliss got up to leave and Sir James did the same. Mrs Grantham bade them a cordial farewell, and assured Fliss of a warm welcome whenever she might choose to drop in. If she was disappointed not to have Sir James to herself at all, she certainly did not show it. Suddenly Fliss wondered whether the welcome was extended to Sir James also, and whether he ever visited Mrs Grantham there alone.

They walked together towards the gates of the manor.

'I trust that Amanda did not distress you with her frank and direct manner,' said Sir James. 'She does not mean any harm, but she does not always know the difference between being interested, and being over-inquisitive.'

'I was a little taken aback,' admitted Fliss, 'but she did not distress me. It is refreshing to have someone new living in the vicinity; I think that she will make an agreeable neighbour.'

'I am glad for her sake that she has someone like yourself nearby, who is prepared to welcome her,' he answered. They soon reached the bottom of the drive, and there Sir James left her, before walking on to Roache Hall.

As Fliss wandered up the drive, she found herself wondering how well he had known Mrs Grantham in London. Certainly well enough for them to be upon first-name terms! It had been through his agency that Mrs Grantham had come into the neighbourhood. Was that only because he had wanted to help an old friend, or was there another, more romantic reason? Suddenly, she recalled how, when she had met Sir James at Brumby's, he had wanted her help in choosing something for a lady friend. Had it been for Mrs Grantham, that he had wanted to buy jewellery? Was it for her that he had bought Grandmama's pendant?

CHAPTER SIX

After Richard's visit, Mrs Wintershill seemed to lose energy, and spent much of the time in bed. Fliss took up the reins of the household and prepared for the arrival of Walter and Wilfred from school and Christopher from Cambridge for Easter.

They all arrived safely amid great excitement, and Christopher was successfully ambushed to the great delight of all concerned. Barbara was very happy to see her twin again. Wilfred and Walter celebrated their arrival by putting a cricket ball through the drawing-room window, so all was felt to be as it should be.

This being the case, Fliss wondered why she should feel so unsettled. Once, she found herself restlessly thumbing through the newspaper which was delivered regularly to Sir James, and which he always passed on to her father. Another time, she realized that for quite ten minutes she had stood staring out of the windows of the long gallery upstairs at nothing in particular. She eventually decided that Mrs Grantham's conversation about Bath and London had reopened her mind to the existence of a wider world in which she could never hope to play a part.

She often wandered in the direction of Christmas Cottage when she was at leisure. Mrs Grantham was always ready to welcome her with a cup of tea, or a glass of wine, and it frequently happened that Sir James joined them. For her part, Fliss found herself feeling a little uncomfortable when he came, and she put this down to anxiety that she might be in the way of a romantic twosome.

One morning, about a week after Christopher's arrival, Fliss was tidying the linen cupboard with Melissa when a message arrived that their father wished to speak to them both in the library. They looked at one another in surprise, took off their aprons, smoothed their hair and went downstairs. They were to be glad that they had taken this trouble, for Sir James was also there. Greatly to her annoyance, Fliss found herself blushing. She had not mentioned the fact that she had seen him so often at Mrs Grantham's house. Now, suddenly, she found herself hoping that he would say nothing of it, for fear that it might sound as if they were indulging in clandestine liaisons.

So busy was she with these thoughts, that she suddenly realized that she was missing everything that her father was saying. She thought that he seemed confused and not a little harassed.

'I will let Sir James explain for himself,' he was saying.

'I have just received a letter from my aunt, who resides in Bath,' said Sir James. He didn't look so overpoweringly big here as he did in Mrs Grantham's tiny room, Fliss thought to herself consideringly. But he towered over her father, and his shoulders were wide . . . Blushing again, she forced herself to listen properly. What on earth was the matter with her today? '. . . lacking in spirits. In order to divert her mind, I had written, telling her a little about your lively family and she was much entertained. She has become very much taken with the idea that two young ladies from your family might go to her for a visit. I am therefore here as her emissary to ask whether you, Miss Wintershill and Miss Melissa, will be so kind as to oblige me by agreeing to visit her?'

Fliss's heart gave a leap before her mind told her how impossible such a venture would be. The whole household depended upon her. How could she get away, now or ever? At the same time, she remembered Sir James's many kindnesses, not just to her, but to the whole family over the past ten years, from allowing the children to run tame over his land, to passing on gifts of fruit and game. Certainly, it must be an object with the family to oblige him if they could.

'Melissa may go if Mama and Papa are in agreement,' she said eventually. 'But what about Barbara instead of myself?'

'I am sure that Miss Barbara would make a charming companion,' Sir James said courteously. 'I believe that she is not out, however. If my aunt is not well, then I fear that the task of chaperoning her might be beyond her powers.'

'And besides,' put in Melissa, 'Fliss is older and will make better company for Sir James's aunt.'

Mr Wintershill pursed his lips. 'Barbara is of an age to come out,' he replied. 'It would be a good opportunity for her to go into society a little. After all, Fliss is now too old to gain full benefit from such a visit.' At these words, Fliss fell something shrivel and die inside her. She swallowed and looked up at Sir James and wondered why his expression should be so angry. Perhaps he was annoyed that they could not agree upon who should go after he had made such a kind offer. He opened his mouth to speak, but before he could say anything, the door into the library, which had been ajar, flew open completely, and Barbara and Christopher stood on the threshold. They really were astonishingly alike with their wavy

53

brown hair, twinkling hazel eyes, and determined chins.

'If Sir James's aunt asked for Fliss, it must have been because it was Fliss that she wanted,' said Barbara decisively. 'And if she wanted to send her guests out on their own, Melissa and I would not be able to go because Melissa is too young to chaperon me.' Sensing a weakening in her father's position, Barbara took a step or two towards him. 'Papa, I know everything that Fliss does, and I can take her place. Chris can help you and do the accounts, at least until he goes back to Cambridge. After a day or two, you'll have forgotten what it was like to have her here.'

Mr Wintershill sighed a little. 'Well, I suppose you had better go and tell your mother,' he said at last.

'Papa!' exclaimed Fliss, and ran to throw her arms around his neck in the manner of a girl half her age. She was also conscious of the desire to do the same to Sir James!

*   *   *

So enthusiastic was Barbara to take charge of the household that Fliss began to wonder whether she would be quite pleased to see her oldest sister go. She ventured to say as much in jest, but Barbara hastened to reassure her.

'Of course not!' she exclaimed. 'I shall miss you dreadfully and be quite envious, but I am relying on you to marry someone rich, so that I can cut a dash in society!'

'If you're hoping for that, then you will have a very long wait,' replied Fliss. 'Lissa is much more likely to oblige you.'

'Perhaps. But don't shrink into the background with all the dowagers,' insisted her masterful sister. 'Remember that Sir James's aunt will be the dowager there.'

Before she left, Fliss visited her new friend at Christmas Cottage. Mrs Grantham was delighted to hear her news, and gave her much the same advice as her sister had done.

'There are plenty of men who would by far rather marry a sensible woman than a silly chit of a girl,' she said. 'You are by no means on the shelf, so don't act as if you are!' Mrs Grantham also bestowed upon Fliss a hair-brown pelisse, which she had bought by mistake, some gloves which had turned out to be the wrong size, and a handsome silk shawl. Fliss accepted the gifts after only a short protest. New things would have to be found for their visit somehow, and very few of them would come cheaply.

Shortly before they were due to leave for Bath, they went to say goodbye to their mother. She was sitting up in bed, but looking so pale and drawn that Fliss almost refused to go. Something of her feeling conveyed itself to Mrs Wintershill, for she said firmly, 'I am so glad that you are both going. I should have

55

made sure that you had a chance before, Fliss; I rather blame myself. But thanks to Sir James's aunt, you are to have that chance now.'

'Mama . . .' began Fliss.

'You are going, and there's an end of it,' said her mother. 'I am not completely useless up here, you know. Barbara can ask me for advice any time she likes. But for now, Lissa, will you pass me that wooden box that is on the chest by the window?' Melissa did as she was bid, and Mrs Wintershill took a smaller box from inside it, and gave it to her. 'They belonged to your father's mother and I had always intended that you should have them some time.' Melissa opened the box, her eyes widening as she took out a delicately fashioned gold necklace with tiny flowers made from sapphires.

'Mama! It's beautiful!' she breathed. 'Are you sure?'

'Quite sure, my dear.' Melissa leaned over to kiss her mother.

'I shall think of you whenever I wear it,' she promised. Mrs Wintershill smiled, and took out another small box, which she handed to Fliss. Fliss opened it to find a diamond bracelet. She stared at it and swallowed convulsively.

'It is the bracelet which goes with Grandmama's pendant,' said her mother. 'I should have given it to you before now.' Then she produced from her box a small velvet bag, which she also handed to her eldest daughter. After a puzzled look, Fliss pulled open the drawstrings of the bag, and upturned it. Onto her hand, to Fliss's stunned amazement, spilled Grandmama's pendant. 'They make a lovely set, don't they?' said her mother, quite unconscious of the consternation that she had caused.

'Y-yes, thank you, Mama,' murmured Fliss, utterly mystified. 'Sir James came up to see me yesterday, to assure me that he would take great care of you both. He had chanced to go into Brumby's and your necklace had been repaired and cleaned more quickly than expected.'

'How . . . how kind,' said Fliss faintly.

'Now, kiss me goodbye, both of you, and promise me that you will have a wonderful time.'

'We will, Mama,' said Melissa, answering for both of them, which was just as well, for Fliss was still too stunned to speak.

'Run along, Lissa, I just want a little word with Fliss,' said Mrs Wintershill. Once Melissa had gone, after bidding her mother an affectionate farewell, she went on, 'I'm glad you will be there with her. Her London experience unsettled her dreadfully. In a smaller place, she may recover her confidence.'

'I'm sure she will. There will be Sir James's

aunt to look after us both, so you mustn't worry.'

'I won't,' promised her mother. 'As long as you assure me that whilst looking after Melissa, you do not neglect your own chances. I am convinced that if you are not stubbornly blind, you will discover the man who is just right for you.' Seeing the pleading light in Mrs Wintershill's eyes, Fliss gave her the assurance she craved and bent to kiss her goodbye. She was about to leave, when she heard her name spoken.

'Yes, Mama?'

'He's a fine man, my dear.' Fliss blushed, smiled uncertainly, and left the room without even asking her mother to whom she was referring.

*   *   *

'What do you suppose Sir James's aunt will be like?' asked Melissa as they travelled. 'I should think that she would be quite old, do not you?' They had received a kind, welcoming letter from Mrs Salisbury, but it had given them no indication of how old she was, or what her state of health or habits might be.

'Why do you think that?' asked Fliss curiously.

'Well, she is Sir James's aunt, isn't she? He is a friend of Papa, and he must be quite old himself.'

'Sir James isn't old,' Fliss answered indignantly as she glanced out of the window. He was riding alongside the carriage as their escort. He had certainly not looked old when he had arrived that morning, impeccably attired in a russet riding coat, buff breeches, and boots so shiny that one might have seen one's face in them. His strong presence was certainly a comfort, she thought as she leaned back against the squabs.

She had not yet had the opportunity to ask him about her necklace. When she had first seen it, her initial thought had been one of delight at seeing it again. Immediately following that had been the realization that Sir James must have paid at least £800 for it. Whilst she could not help but be relieved that it was not to adorn the neck of Mrs Grantham, or of any other female of Sir James's acquaintance, she knew that she would have to confront him about it and offer to pay the sum back—though how that was ever to be accomplished was anyone's guess. Whatever might happen on that score, however, she could not help but be touched by the delicacy with which he had returned the necklace without disclosing how he had acquired it. Mama was right: he was a fine man, and she was only just beginning to realize it. A slight jolt in the road brought her out of her mood of abstraction. She glanced across at Melissa and saw that she was smiling.

'What is so amusing?' she asked defensively. 'Nothing!' replied Melissa innocently, the smile disappearing at once. 'I was just thinking how fortunate we are that Sir James has lent us his chaise to travel in.' To this Fliss was obliged to agree. They were undoubtedly very comfortable in Sir James's well-sprung chaise.

The journey was not a long one, for they lived only two hours from Bath. The spring day was fine and the roads were good, being neither muddy nor dusty. As they drew closer to Bath, the road started to climb, and Fliss found it very hard to contain her excitement.

'Really, Fliss,' said Melissa, with all the superiority of one who had enjoyed a London season, 'anyone would think that you were a girl in her teens!'

'I feel like it,' said Fliss, turning to her sister, her eyes shining. 'I feel so . . . so'—she searched her mind for the right word and eventually simply whispered, 'free.'

Mrs Salisbury lived in Laura Place, and by the time they drew up outside her door at almost exactly half past eleven, even Melissa had abandoned her air of knowledgeability, and both of them had been hard put to tear themselves away from the windows. Only the fear of appearing like yokels enabled them to retain some sense of decorum.

On their arrival, Sir James sprang down from his horse in order to hand them down from the carriage. Fliss, unaware of how much the excitement enhanced her complexion, turned a glowing face up to him as she thanked him. He looked at her with approval.

'Travel agrees with you, Miss Wintershill,' he remarked. 'You are looking uncommonly well.' She could not help thinking the same thing about him, for the exercise had given his cheeks a healthy ruddiness, although naturally she did not say so.

The party was clearly expected, for the door was thrown open and they were ushered inside immediately by the butler. 'Good morning, Yare,' said Sir James. 'I hope I see you well?'

'Thank you, Sir James, I am very well indeed. I will inform Mrs Salisbury that you have arrived safely with the young ladies.' They followed the butler across the neat, light hall and up the stairs to the drawing-room door, which he opened, after which he announced them all.

'James!' cried a surprisingly youthful voice and, as they all entered the room, they saw Sir James being embraced by a lady who was clearly no older than himself. 'My dear, this is wonderful indeed! I did not expect you until dinner-time! And you have brought my two welcome house-guests, who are going to charm me out of my ennui!'

'I'm sure they will do their best,' replied Sir James, disentangling himself from her embrace. 'But allow me to present them first. Elvira, this is Miss Wintershill and her sister,

Miss Melissa Wintershill. Ladies, allow me to introduce to you my aunt, Mrs Salisbury.'

Fliss and Melissa made their curtsies and murmured something polite, but they were clearly looking somewhat bemused, for Mrs Salisbury gave another of her very attractive tinkling laughs and said, 'Oh, how shocking! James has not told you anything about me, and you have been imagining me to be a very old lady! Do not deny it, for I can see it in your faces!'

Fliss could not help laughing. 'You're very perceptive, ma'am,' she said. 'It is quite true that when Sir James asked us to come and bear his aunt company, he gave us no indication that she would be so young and attractive.'

'James, she is delightful,' cried Mrs Salisbury, clapping her hands. 'I can feel my ennui disappearing already! Come with me both of you, and I will show you to your rooms. James, ring for some wine, if you please. We shall be down directly.' Fliss and Melissa followed their hostess with a sense of pleasurable anticipation, for one happy word had caught the ear and the imagination of both of them and that word was 'rooms'. Could it really be true that they were to have a room each?

It could. Fliss was shown into a delightful room with blue curtains and bed hangings to match, and a thick carpet with not a single threadbare patch in sight. There was a communicating door between the two rooms, and no sooner had Mrs Salisbury left them, than Melissa flew through the door, and he sisters embraced, exclaiming almost simultaneously, 'A room each! How wonderful!'

'Fliss, I just know that we are going to have a wonderful time here,' breathed Melissa, her eyes shining. Fliss smiled back, and squeezed her sister's hands.

It did not take them long to tidy themselves up, and they soon returned to the drawing-room to join their hostess and her nephew. Despite being closely related, they were not at all alike. The baronet towered over his aunt who was small and plump, with a head of golden curls, and cornflower-blue eyes. She was fashionably dressed in a pale-blue morning gown with a muslin ruff edged with lace. After Sir James had poured wine for everyone, Mrs Salisbury, said, 'Now let me explain matters! James's grandfather—my father—married early. His son, James's father, was born in the first year of their marriage, but after that there were no more children until, twenty years later, I was born, not just in the same year as James, but in the same month and on the same day as well! We grew up almost as twin brother and sister, although I am his aunt.'

'What an amazing story,' commented Fliss.

'Sir James gave us no hint at all that you were the same age.'

'I expect he did it to tease you,' said her hostess, looking at the unrepentant baronet with a mock severe expression. 'I am afraid that James can be something of a rogue.' A rogue! That was not a term that Fliss had ever thought of applying to her father's friend! 'And I will tell you something even worse; he does not seem to be able to show me the proper deference and respect!'

'It's shameful, ma'am,' smiled Fliss.

'It is indeed. But I must not abuse him, for he takes very good care of me and has come to my rescue on more than one occasion.' Fliss glanced across at the baronet. She could not help thinking that she could say much the same thing. 'Where are you putting up, James?' went on his aunt.

'At the Christopher. I have commitments at home, and am not sure how long I shall stay.'

'Well, do not rush off. It is very agreeable to have a gentleman's escort, is it not, ladies?' Melissa and Fliss readily agreed.

That evening, Sir James dined with them in Laura Place, and a very pleasant evening they had of it. For the first time in a very long period, Fliss found herself able to enjoy the meal and the surroundings, without feeling in any way responsible for the arrangements. Mrs Salisbury and her nephew were both very careful not to indulge in prolonged conversations in which the sisters could not join, but from the remarks that passed between them from time to time, Fliss realized that they both inhabited a world in which she had hardly taken part. She looked at Sir James seated at the head of the table, faultlessly turned out in the black and silver evening dress that he had worn once at Wintershill Court. He looked every inch the man of the world.

After dinner, Sir James declined to sit alone, and brought his glass of brandy through to the drawing-room, where Melissa was invited to play for them on the piano.

'Your sister plays delightfully,' remarked Mrs Salisbury.

'Yes, I think she is the most accomplished of the family,' replied Fliss.

'And do you play, Miss Wintershill?'

Fliss shook her head. 'I am not at all accomplished,' she replied smiling.

'Miss Wintershill is too slighting of her own talents,' said Sir James, surprising her. 'Her gifts lie in taking the burdens from other people's shoulders.' Fliss looked at him for a long moment before blushing and looking away.

After Sir James had gone, and Melissa, pleading tiredness, had gone up to bed—to revel, Fliss was convinced, in having a room to herself—Mrs Salisbury said to Fliss, 'Pray don't go up just yet, Miss Wintershill, unless you are really fatigued from your journey. I would like to talk to you for a little while.' To tell the truth, Fliss was not feeling at all tired. The adventure of coming to Bath to a new situation had so stimulated her that she did not feel in the least bit exhausted, so she readily came to sit down next to her hostess. 'Ever since I knew that you would be coming I have been making plans,' went on Mrs Salisbury confidentially. 'I have no more daughters to bring out, you see, so I am very much looking forward to taking you about and finding husbands for you both!'

'Not for me, ma'am,' said Fliss, colouring. 'I am long past my last prayers. If anything could be done for Lissa, it would be wonderful, but . . .' She drew a breath. 'We have no money, you see—or at any rate, none to speak of.' Mrs Salisbury waved her hand dismissively.

'That need not be a problem,' she said. 'Remember, you have lived very retired. Here in a wider society, you will find that people are not so ruled by a woman's age, or even by her lack of her portion, unless she allows it to be so. But whatever happens, my dear Miss Wintershill, we shall certainly have fun!'

CHAPTER SEVEN

The fun began the following day when Mrs Salisbury declared that they would go shopping. It was a long time since Melissa and Fliss had browsed among the shops simply for pleasure. Their shopping usually consisted of buying essential articles in the village, or sometimes in Marlborough.

On this occasion, however, they were to be doing a little more than just looking into the shop windows, or even observing Mrs Salisbury spend her money without being able to spend any of their own. Fliss had retained the hundred pounds from her portion and was determined to use it wisely. It could well be that Mrs Salisbury was right about Bath. It was smaller than London but with a society more varied than that which was to be found in their own area, and there might just be a chance to find a husband for Melissa, but Fliss knew that she was woefully ignorant concerning fashions and society ways. With these things in mind, she took her hostess on one side and explained their situation.

'Of course, my dear, I understand perfectly,' said Mrs Salisbury soothingly. 'No one loves a bargain better than I and it is entirely true to say that if one strays out of Milsom Street, one can often find something just as good for half the money!'

At first inclined to protest, Melissa allowed herself to be persuaded into having three new gowns: a walking dress in blue, a day dress in a paler shade, and an evening gown of white muslin. Fliss would only have purchased a single evening gown for herself, but Mrs Salisbury strongly urged her to purchase more, for, as she said, 'What is the good of Melissa going round looking as fine as fivepence, whilst you are standing next to her looking shabby?' So, for Melissa's sake—or so Fliss told herself—she chose a walking dress in bronze and an evening gown in primrose yellow. With the addition of sundry other items, such as shawls, bonnets and gloves, all bought by Mrs Salisbury's recommendation in Stall Street rather than Milsom Street, Melissa and Fliss felt as if they could hold up their heads in any company.

Later that day, as Fliss was helping Melissa to do up her gown, Mrs Salisbury appeared, followed by her abigail who was carrying some material over her arm.

'Look what Simpson has found!' she exclaimed. 'Laura—my daughter, you know— left these behind when she got married, and I am sure that there is very little difference between her and Melissa! What do you think, Simpson?' Simpson cast a knowledgeable eye over both of the sisters.

'Nothing at all between Miss Laura and

68

Miss Melissa, I'd say, ma'am,' she replied. 'But I'll need to take something off the length for Miss Wintershill.' The girls tried to protest, but were quickly over-ruled.

'What do you think I should do with them if you don't have them?' asked their hostess.

'Perhaps your daughter will want them,' ventured Fliss.

'If she had wanted them, she would have taken them when she left,' said Mrs Salisbury positively. 'Now, say no more, for it is settled, and Simpson will do any alterations, will you not, Simpson?'

'With pleasure, ma'am.'

'You must wear them tomorrow, for we are going to the Pump Room and, as you probably know already, that is the place to see and be seen. And we must also make sure that you go to both assembly rooms and sign the subscription books—every fashionable visitor does, you know.'

Thanks to Simpson's skill, the Wintershill sisters found themselves feeling very elegant the following day, Melissa in a pink round gown with a cross-over front, and Fliss in a green gown with a low square neck, which flustered her a little, until Mrs Salisbury assured her that it was perfectly decent.

'You look quite charming, my dear,' she declared. 'Be quite certain that I would not tell you so if it were not true!' When they arrived at the Pump Room and saw the quantities of

69

elegant people strolling to and fro, Fliss found herself agreeing with her hostess on the fashionable nature of the place. There were a number of sick and elderly people about, but, in general, they were outnumbered by very healthy-looking individuals, most of whom were clearly there for the social benefits to be gained. Fliss was very relieved to see that there were a number of women wearing gowns that were lower cut than the one she was wearing, so she stopped worrying about it and prepared to enjoy herself.

As soon as they arrived, Mrs Salisbury began greeting people that she knew, and, moments later, Melissa exclaimed, 'There is Ruth Stringer! I met her in London. Do you mind if I go over and speak to her?' Fliss shook her head, and was about to join Mrs Salisbury, who was in conversation with an elderly woman in a great hooped skirt of a rich purple hue, when she saw Sir James approaching her, and she remembered that she had still not had an opportunity to speak to him about her necklace. Dressed in a green cloth coat and dull gold waistcoat, his hair neatly tied back with a ribbon, he looked as fine as any gentleman there.

'Good morning, Sir James,' she said, curtsying politely in response to his elegant bow. 'You see us where all Bath is this morning, I believe—but we have not yet braved the waters!'

'Then allow me to assist you, ma'am,' he replied with a twinkle. 'It wants but a little courage! Shall we walk?'

As they moved towards the place where attendants were helping people to the water, she said, 'Sir James, I must thank you for your kindness once again.'

'For introducing you to the water?' he asked quizzically. 'Wait till you've tasted it! You may want to retract your words.'

'No indeed,' replied Fliss. She paused, then went on, 'I think you cannot be unaware of what my grandmother's necklace means to me.'

'Ah,' said Sir James.

'You have been kind enough to return it to me—at heaven knows what cost! How can I thank you . . . or repay you?' He stopped walking, and laid his hand briefly upon hers before releasing it.

'I suggest you cease to trouble yourself with such thoughts,' he replied. 'It was my pleasure to restore it to its proper owner.'

'But the extra money—that must have been from you, too. Sir James, I cannot . . .'

'Listen to me,' he said in a serious and compelling tone. 'Your family has been kindness itself to me since William and I came to live at Roache Hall. How could I withhold something which would help you and which was in my power to give?'

She did not reply at once, but eventually she

murmured, 'Such kindness deserves an explanation, but I cannot give one without . . .' She halted, aware that even by these few words she might be running the risk of betraying Richard.

'Enough,' he said firmly but kindly. 'My acquaintance with you is sufficient for me to be assured that your motives are honourable ones.' Seeing her worried look, he added, 'You are still anxious, but it is not necessary.' He smiled wryly. 'Call it an early bridal gift.'

'It will have to be repaid, for I shall not marry,' she said matter-of-factly. Then she went on in a more moved tone, 'But I am grateful to you for the way in which you returned it so that my mother should not be aware of . . . of the situation. The delicacy with which you acted . . .' He made a disclaiming gesture, but said nothing. They walked together in silence for a while, then Fliss began again. 'I owe you another debt as well.'

Sir James shook his head. 'No more gratitude, I beg of you, ma'am,' he said laughing. 'I find it far too wearing!'

'Just one more thing I must mention, by your leave,' begged Fliss. 'Sir, you know as well as I that your aunt is not ill, and Melissa and I appear to be here chiefly for our own pleasure!' He was silent for a moment.

'Very well then, Miss Wintershill,' he declared eventually. 'Since you are so intent on expressing your gratitude, there is a way in which you can show it to me. But perhaps,' he added provocatively 'you are not sincere in your profession.'

She could not think what he might ask, so she replied, 'Of course I am sincere. And certainly I am prepared to show my gratitude, as long as . . . that is . . .' Her voice faded away.

'Don't look so anxious, Miss Wintershill,' he said with a teasing note in his voice. His eyes had a twinkle that was decidedly roguish. 'Surely you do not think that I am about to ask for something improper!'

Encouraged by his tone, she answered him in like manner, 'Certainly not here in the Pump Room, sir!' Why, he is flirting with me, she thought to herself. And what is more, *I* am flirting with *him*!

He laughed, and said, 'It is just that it would give me great pleasure if when you address me, you would drop my title, and call me by my Christian name, and if you would allow me to be similarly informal when I speak to you.'

'You want me to call you simply James?'

'No, no, that would be even worse!' he protested, laughing. 'If you feel you cannot fall in with my request, then stick to "Sir James". Somehow, I find that "Simply James" goes very much against the grain.' Fliss laughed as well, then.

'It will seem strange,' she said thoughtfully after they had stopped laughing. 'After all, you are a friend of my father.'

73

The baronet sighed ruefully. 'Miss Wintershill, do you know that you have an unequalled capacity for making me feel old?'

'No, do I? I beg your pardon! I did not mean to do so for I don't think of you as old at all.' As she said the words, she realized that she was not just saying them to be polite, but that she actually meant them.

'You relieve me extremely. But now, to prove my point: your father reliably informs me that in mathematics you are the expert of the family. So answer me this: your father is sixty; you, I believe, are twenty-five; I am forty-one. To which of the two of you am I closest in age?'

'Oh,' murmured Fliss. She had never considered that Sir James and her father might be of different generations. 'Very well then—James,' she said a little shyly. 'But you must be patient with me if I slip up from time to time.'

'Of course I will—Felicity,' he answered. She stared up at him. It only occurred to her later how strange it should be that the full form of her name on his lips should sound so much more intimate than the informal, family version would have done.

'No one calls me that,' she said. She was not angry, only a little puzzled.

'I've noticed,' he said drily. 'You have a beautiful name, which nobody uses. Do you dislike it so very much?'

'I don't dislike it at all,' she confessed. 'It is

just that everyone shortens it to Fliss. My grandmother always called me by my full name and I liked it, but after she died, no one did.'

'May I do so?' he asked her gently.

'Yes . . . yes, you may,' she said quietly, feeling absurdly shy.

'Thank you. And now, Felicity, I see that our wanderings have brought us back to the vicinity of the famous water. I think that you should demonstrate your trust in me by drinking a glass of it!' Fliss took the glass from the attendant, and obediently drank it straight away, whilst it was still warm, so as to get the maximum benefit. The expression on her face made Sir James laugh.

'It is all very well for you to be so amused,' she said severely. 'You have not drunk any!'

'No, that is true,' he agreed as he led her back to his aunt, who was now standing with Melissa and two other ladies. 'You see, I had tasted it before!' When they had rejoined the other members of their party, Melissa begged leave to present her friend Ruth Stringer, who was visiting Bath with her aunt. Ruth was much the same height as Melissa, but with a more angular figure, ginger hair, and rather prominent teeth. Her aunt professed herself delighted to meet Ruth's friends.

'For you must know, Miss Wintershill, that she has talked so much about her friend Melissa and her charming family!' Fliss murmured gratification at this intelligence, although she could not recall that Ruth's affection for Melissa had resulted in a single letter. She also found it interesting that Mrs Makepiece seemed to be even more delighted to meet Sir James. 'How agreeable it will be to have a gentleman with whom we are acquainted in Bath, will it not, Ruth?' Ruth blushingly agreed.

'Sadly, matters of business will take me away,' said Sir James courteously. 'But I look forward to hearing how you are enjoying your visit.' Mrs Makepiece smiled, but less expansively than before.

After they had left the Pump Room, Mrs Salisbury said to Melissa, 'How agreeable for you to have found an old friend in Bath, my dear.'

Melissa smiled and murmured something in agreement, but later, when she and Fliss were alone, she admitted, 'I didn't really like her. We met quite frequently, but we didn't have that much in common.'

The following day, Sir James returned home and they did not see him for nearly a week. During his absence, they visited the Pump Room nearly every day, and attended worship in the Abbey, as well as visiting both assembly rooms and signing the subscription books. Mr Tyson and Mr King, the two masters of ceremonies, both called and were very civil, and Fliss suspected that this was probably in deference to Mrs Salisbury. They often saw

Ruth Stringer and her aunt, but they did not become close.

It soon dawned upon Fliss that Sir James was widely regarded as an eligible and personable gentleman. Of course he had a title and fortune, but more than this, his stature and confident demeanour, combined with his elegant dress, and faultless manners, made him an agreeable companion and desirable escort. After he had returned to Roache Hall, more than one lady managed to enquire about him in a roundabout way.

Six days after Sir James's departure, Fliss and Melissa were returning to Laura Place after a morning walk. The breeze was fresh, and had whipped colour into their cheeks. They were about to mount the steps when a voice attracted their attention and, turning, they saw Sir James getting down off his horse.

'Well met, ladies!' he declared, in high good humour as he handed the reins over to his groom. 'You are both looking remarkably well. It must be all that beneficial water from the Pump Room!' His remarks were addressed to both of them, but it was on Fliss's face that his admiring gaze rested for the longest.

'It must be the lack of it that is doing us good, then,' replied Fliss, 'for we have both been carefully avoiding it! Will you not come in, sir?'

He accepted her invitation, but, as he stood back for them, he murmured under his breath,

'My name is James,' unaccountably causing Fliss's heart to miss a beat. Yare conducted him to the drawing-room and brought him some wine whilst they were putting off their bonnets. When Fliss got downstairs, she found Sir James alone, sipping the wine that had been brought for him.

'Your sister has not yet come down, and I am told that my aunt is visiting a friend,' he said. 'May I pour for you?' Fliss assented, and took the glass from him with a word of thanks.

'Have you seen anything of my family?' she asked him.

'I have,' he replied. 'I rode over yesterday, knowing that you would be glad of any news. Miss Barbara is ruling the household with great dash and enthusiasm. Christopher has been adding up huge columns of figures, but has discovered that he is not as good at it as you are. He is frequently finding pennies going astray.'

'That may be Papa's writing,' remarked Fliss. 'It is not always very clear.'

'I will remember to tell him next time I go. The younger ones seem to be in fine health.' He paused for a moment. 'I did not see your mother, but I believe that she is not well at present.'

'Oh dear,' murmured Fliss a little anxiously. 'I wonder whether I should—'

'Certainly not,' said James in an authoritative tone. 'She is well cared for and your presence would neither relieve her nor make her worse.'

'But you must allow me to have a little family feeling,' she said gently.

'Your life has been ruled by little else,' he replied, his tone rather irritable. 'I suppose I should not be surprised that it is coming to the surface yet again.'

'Of course you should not be surprised,' she retorted indignantly. 'Am I not entitled to be concerned for my mother?'

'Yes, you are entitled to be concerned. But recall, if you please, that it was your mother's wish that you should come to Bath. All I am saying is that you need to have a sense of proportion.'

'A sense of proportion!' she declared exasperatedly. 'Since when has it been possible to contain one's emotions in that kind of way?'

He looked at her steadily for a long moment, then said, 'You are right of course; it is not possible.'

She went on as if he had said nothing, 'Just because you have no one to worry about—'

'That is untrue and a little unfair,' he said mildly. Suddenly realizing how she had been speaking to him without restraint, she coloured deeply.

'I beg your pardon,' she said in mortified tones. 'I do not understand why I am quarrelling with you in this way.'

'What is a disagreement between friends?'

he said and smiled. Suddenly, Fliss remembered her mother saying that he was a fine man. Before she could pursue these thoughts any further, the door opened and Melissa came in. 'By the way,' he went on, 'Amanda Grantham sends you both her love and asks me to tell you that you are under strict instructions to enjoy yourselves prodigiously whilst you are here.'

'How kind of her,' said Melissa. 'But you may tell her when next you see her, Sir James, that we are enjoying ourselves already. Are we not, Fliss?' Fliss agreed, but she could not help wondering whether he had met Mrs Grantham by chance or had sought her out.

It was one of the excitements of Bath that the arrival of important visitors was announced by a peal of bells, so, when one morning the bells were sounded, the ladies of Laura Place could not help wondering whose arrival might be heralded. An acquaintance of Mrs Salisbury, a Mrs Foreshore by name, came round especially with the news.

'I understand it is some members of the family of the Duke of Brigham,' she told them. 'Should one say "it is" or "they are", I wonder? I'm not sure. Anyway, it is not the duke, so I understand, although I think he did come here once and didn't like it much, although why he should not do so is a mystery to me, for I find it very agreeable. No, I believe it is just ladies in the party, a daughter of his, or it could be a daughter-in-law, and her family, and I believe they are to take a house quite near to you, dear Mrs Salisbury, in Laura Place, so you will have an agreeable neighbour. That is, if she is agreeable, but of course there is the chance that she may not be. After all, being a duke's daughter is no guarantee of anything, is it?' The ladies could find nothing to argue with in this, and as Mrs Foreshore had no further information to impart, she did not stay for longer than another quarter of an hour, talking continuously until the moment of her departure. Mrs Salisbury smiled ruefully at Fliss after she had gone.

'You will be wondering, I expect, why I tolerate such an irrepressible chatterer,' she said.

'I would not dream of being so uncivil,' replied Fliss. 'But she does talk rather a lot.'

'Yes, and sometimes it is quite tempting, if one is not feeling very talkative oneself, to just allow it to flow over one.'

Later, Melissa said to her sister, 'These people must be relations of Lord Octavius, I suppose. I wonder if they will be agreeable?'

'Well, according to Mrs Foreshore, their relationship to the Duke of Brigham can be no guarantee of that,' said Fliss playfully. Then she went on, 'Lord Octavius certainly was though, wasn't he? So perhaps they will be, also.' Melissa agreed, but quite unselfconsciously, so Fliss decided that

81

perhaps she had not been so taken with the handsome naval officer after all.

The new arrivals made their first appearance the following day in the Pump Room. They were the Lady Susan Tryon who was Octavius's older sister, and her daughter Alice. Lady Susan, a tall, vigorous-looking woman in her late thirties, quite dwarfed her daughter, who was small, slim and quiet. Mrs Salisbury, who appeared to know almost everybody, greeted Lady Susan with pleasure, and begged leave to introduce her two guests. Her Ladyship was pleased to be gracious. She recalled meeting Mrs Wintershill when she had been Miss Summers, and detected in Melissa a distinct likeness to her mother. She would be very pleased if Melissa would conduct her to the water and procure her a glass. Melissa was glad to oblige, and walked away with Lady Susan, leaving Fliss and Mrs Salisbury to converse with Miss Tryon.

'Is this your first visit to Bath, Miss Tryon?' asked Fliss.

'Yes . . . I mean no, I came last year.'

'And are you staying in the same house?'

'Yes.'

'It must almost seem like coming home.'

'Yes, it does.'

Fliss was beginning to wonder for how much longer she could continue this laboured conversation when Mrs Salisbury turned away to speak to someone else. Immediately, Alice's manner underwent a surprising change. More animation came into her face; she gained colour and said rapidly in a low tone, 'Miss Wintershill, forgive my presumption, but I must ask you while I have the chance. Pray tell me, is your name Fliss?'

Until a few days ago, Fliss would have said 'Yes'. Now, she found herself saying, 'That is not really my name, but it is what most of my family call me.'

'Then I know I can speak freely to you. Richard told me I could.'

'Richard . . .' murmured Fliss, not quite understanding where this conversation might be leading.

'Yes, Richard,' repeated Alice with an impatient note in her voice which was quite at variance with her earlier reserved manner. 'We must talk, but it is not possible here, for Mama will return at any moment.' She wrinkled her brow, then her expression lightened and she said, 'I know! Meet me in the Sydney Gardens at two o'clock.' Fliss did not have time to answer, for Lady Susan and Melissa rejoined them at that moment. Fliss looked at Miss Tryon and saw that she had returned to being the meek little mouse that she had been before. Lady Susan laughed indulgently.

'I am afraid that Alice is so shy, Miss Wintershill, that she can never converse with anyone with ease.' Fliss glanced at Miss Tryon, who looked up at her briefly, and cast her a glance that was full of meaning. Fliss nodded almost imperceptibly and in response to Lady Susan, smiled and said something non-committal. It seemed to her that meek and mild little Alice might be able to teach her forthright mother a thing or two, given the opportunity.

CHAPTER EIGHT

Fliss had been a little concerned that she would have to find an excuse for getting away from Melissa and Mrs Salisbury that afternoon, but this proved unnecessary. Mrs Salisbury decided to go upstairs for a nap, and Melissa had received an invitation from Ruth Stringer to go shopping.

'I thought you didn't like her,' commented Fliss.

'No, I don't really,' replied Melissa frankly. 'But the family are very accustomed to society. To have their acquaintance may be helpful to Barbara when she comes out.'

'Yes, but don't punish yourself too much,' said Fliss.

'I won't,' promised Melissa, laughing.

Once Fliss had put on her bonnet, she went downstairs, carefully avoiding Yare, and letting herself quietly out of the house. Yare was an old family retainer who had soon begun to take a fatherly interest in the Wintershill ladies, and she would not have put it past him to insist that she take a maid or footman with her. Once safely outside, she walked confidently down Great Pulteney Street. After all, it was only a step from Laura Place to the Sydney Gardens, and she was a woman of twenty-five, not a mere slip of a girl.

Fliss had never seen the gardens by night, when, on occasions, they were enhanced by fireworks, cascades and coloured lanterns, but they were pretty enough during the day, with their shady trees, pleasant walkways and refreshing water features. She was perfectly happy to walk about for some time, simply enjoying the fresh air and the happy situation of the gardens. When half an hour had passed, however, she began to realize the equivocal nature of her situation. A rather disreputable-looking gentleman was eyeing her with interest, and she was just thinking that she would have to return to Laura Place without seeing Alice, when that lady herself hurried over, accompanied by her maid.

'Please forgive me! I am so late!' she exclaimed. 'Mama would not leave me alone! She can be so annoying at times. Shall we walk?' They began to walk along together, the maid falling discreetly behind. 'I am so glad to be able to speak openly,' went on Alice. 'I want to talk about Richard with you, and ask for your help.' Fliss looked at her and smiled.

'What is it?' asked Alice.

'Miss Tryon, forgive me for saying so, but I really must tell you that the contrast between your manner yesterday when I first met you and your manner today is most marked.'

Alice smiled ruefully. 'Mama can be very forceful at times, and I discovered a long time ago that the easiest thing is to let her have her head. But we must get down to business, for I cannot be absent for too long. Tell me, Miss Wintershill, what do you know about Richard and myself?' Fliss hesitated, reluctant to betray a confidence without her brother's express permission. 'I can tell that you are not sure whether you can trust me,' said Alice. 'Well, I know that I can trust you for Richard told me so. Richard and I met after some sort of naval display at Portsmouth. My Uncle Tavy brought him when he came to join us for dinner at the Crown. Miss Wintershill, have you ever met someone and known straight away that they would be special to you?'

'No, never,' admitted Fliss. 'Was that how it was with you and Richard?' Alice nodded. Fliss remembered that Richard, in describing his first meeting with Alice, had said something very similar.

'We met a few more times and those meetings only confirmed our attraction to one another. Then Mama and I returned to Brigham and Richard and Tavy had to stay with their ship. I'm not sure what I thought would happen then. I think that we both wanted to see whether what we had felt was a lasting attachment.

'After we had been at Brigham for a short time, Mama decided that she wished to consult her physician, so we returned to London. Whilst we were there, Tavy and Richard arrived. We only had to see one another again, Miss Wintershill, for us both to know that we must be together, but we have a problem.'

'Money?' ventured Fliss.

'Exactly so,' agreed Alice. 'Is it not absurd, Miss Wintershill, that one is not supposed to speak about money for fear of being thought vulgar; yet one must think about it, save it, and even marry it wherever possible!'

Fliss laughed. 'I have never thought of it in that way, but you are absolutely right, Miss Tryon.'

'We are not a wealthy family. Papa frittered away all the money he had, and although Mama puts on airs we are always scrimping and saving. She has always intended me to marry someone with ample means, and, until I met Richard, I thought that I would be able to be obedient to her wishes. Now, I do not see how I can. Oh Miss Wintershill, what am I to do?'

'Is there no one in your family, or close to you, who would take your part?' Fliss asked her.

'I did wonder about my grandfather, the

duke,' replied Alice. 'But he is as anxious to get money into the family as anyone else, if not more so. When we were at Brigham and Mama started to talk about Mr Paranforth, a wealthy gentleman who seemed as if he might be interested in me, he urged me to encourage him all I could, because it would be the saving of us!' She paused for a moment, then laid her hand on Fliss's arm. 'Can you not send for Richard?' she asked. 'Is he at home now?'

'You must remember that I have been away from home for some days,' replied Fliss. 'He might be there but I would not know it.'

'Please!' cried Alice beseechingly. 'Can you not try? Mama has heard that Mr Paranforth is to come to Bath—indeed, that is why we have come here—and if he does so and declares himself, I don't know what I shall do!'

Fliss thought for a moment. 'I shall write to Barbara and ask if he is at home,' she promised at last, 'but I do not really have any knowledge of his movements.' In a more cheerful tone, she went on, 'Try not to be too despondent. All manner of things might happen to change this situation.'

'I don't suppose Richard has a wealthy uncle who might die and leave him his fortune?' said Alice tentatively.

'I'm afraid not,' answered Fliss, reflecting that it would have to be a very big fortune indeed if it could be shared between fifteen of them and still be worth anything.

'No, neither have I,' returned Alice despondently. The two ladies walked back to Laura Place together, by mutual consent talking now of indifferent topics until they parted at Mrs Salisbury's door.

Fliss wished that she could have shared this problem with someone else, but without Alice's permission, she did not feel justified in doing so. She supposed that in all honesty she ought to send a letter to Wintershill Court as she had agreed, even though she was virtually certain that Richard would not be there.

She was still wondering what to do next day as the three of them were preparing to go to the Pump Room. They were on the point of leaving, when there was a knock at the door, and Yare opened it to reveal Sir James standing on the threshold.

'I returned from Roache Hall late last night and hazarded a guess that you might be leaving for the Pump Room at about now. Am I right?'

'Exactly right!' exclaimed Mrs Salisbury. What a fortunate circumstance! You may escort us, James.'

'I should be delighted,' he replied, then acknowledged the other two ladies. 'Felicity, Miss Melissa.' Melissa looked a little surprised, for Fliss had not told her about James's request that they call one another by their Christian names, but Fliss did not notice her expression, for James was smiling at her and she found herself smiling back. As the two sisters walked along behind Sir James and Mrs Salisbury—to whom he had offered his arm— Fliss remembered the problem of Alice and Richard. She had still not sent a message home about her brother, and she wondered what she ought to do. As she looked at Sir James's well-built figure, she knew a longing to confide in him, but she was aware that she could not do this without the permission of those most closely concerned.

In the event, the problem was solved in the most unexpected way. They had not been in the Pump Room for more than a few minutes when to her great surprise she saw her brother Richard approaching them accompanied by Octavius Bonsor. She turned to her sister saying, 'Good heavens! It is Richard!'

To her amazement, Melissa had lost nearly all her colour and was looking as if she might faint. The two officers hurried forward and Richard helped her to a chair, whilst Lord Octavius looked on concernedly. Whilst all this activity was going on, Richard found a moment to say to Fliss, 'Alice is here, isn't she? Have you seen her, and spoken to her?'

'Yes, I have,' answered Fliss, a little irritated by Richard's apparent lack of concern for his sister. 'But at the moment, Melissa is my first concern. Stay with her, Richard, whilst I procure a glass of water for her.' She took a few steps forward, then Octavius caught up with her and said, 'Allow me.' Fliss thanked him, and was about to return to Melissa when she realized that Sir James, unaware of what had occurred, was trying to catch her eye. He was talking to another gentleman, and he appeared to be in high good humour. Looking round, she saw that Richard, acting on her instructions, was sitting with his sister, who appeared to be a little better, so she walked over to Sir James and his companion.

'Felicity, allow me to present to you a friend of mine, Lord Nicholas Bonsor. Nick, this is Miss Wintershill who, along with her sister, has been kind enough to stay with Elvira.' Felicity made her curtsy, and looked up at Lord Nicholas. He was about the same height as Sir James, and of much the same sort of build, although perhaps a little slimmer. His likeness to Octavius was remarkable, but the years that separated them had clearly not been well spent, for Lord Nick's hair was white at the temples, and his face was deeply riven with lines of dissipation. Fliss realized that she was seeing a dangerous rake at close quarters, and she wondered why such men could ever be thought attractive. Then, observing her scrutiny, he grinned at her. It was a somewhat crooked, even lopsided grin, and finding herself smiling back at him, she wondered no longer.

'Miss Wintershill, I am delighted to make your acquaintance,' he said in what could only be described as a seductive drawl. 'I'm pleased to see that Elvira has not yet driven you mad— but beware, it may yet come!'

'Mrs Salisbury has been very kind,' replied Fliss. 'May I assume that you are a brother of Lieutenant Bonsor, Lord Nicholas?'

'Lord Nick will do,' he answered, 'otherwise, I'll think I'm in disgrace, and I haven't been back in the country for long enough to get into mischief! Yes, I'm one of Tavy's older brothers.' He grinned impishly. 'I'm the member of the family that no one talks about. What Susan'll do when she discovers that I'm here I dread to think.'

'I'm sure you exaggerate, my Lord,' said Fliss politely. Stealing a glance at Sir James, she noticed that he did not appear to be in as good a humour as he had when the conversation had begun.

'Believe me I don't,' retorted Lord Nick. 'When I went abroad, they thought they'd seen the last of me, only to have their hopes confounded when I returned this week. There's very little love lost between some of us.'

'But you have come straight to Bath, where three members of your family are staying,' pointed out Fliss. 'I protest, my Lord, you must have more family affection than you are admitting!'

'Ah, but you see, I didn't come to see them at all; I came to see Solitaire.'

92

'Solitaire?' asked Fliss, wrinkling her brow.

'Miss Wintershill is not conversant with my old nickname,' said Sir James hurriedly, 'and I beg that you will not enlighten her.' Nick's grin widened into a wicked smile.

'My dear James!' he protested. 'Miss Wintershill is an intelligent woman! I hardly need to explain to her that your nickname is simply a poetic version of your surname! But, ma'am,'—and here he lowered his voice confidentially—'there is another reason, which is . . .'

'Nick,' said James warningly, 'if you have a fancy to keep your skin whole, you'll stop there.' His tone was light, but his expression seemed to Fliss to carry a hint of anxiety .

'. . . that he was used to wear in his cravat a particularly fine diamond!' completed Lord Nick. Then he went on irrepressibly, 'Why, James, you almost look relieved. What did you think I was going to say?'

'What I will say, Nick, is that you haven't changed one iota,' said Sir James. The two men exchanged a long glance, and Fliss gained the impression that they were both recalling many memories. Suddenly she recalled Melissa's spell of faintness, and exclaimed, 'My sister! She was not feeling well. I must attend her immediately.' She turned round, but Melissa and Richard had both gone. Before she had time to become anxious, Lord Octavius came towards them.

'It's all right,' he said smiling. 'Richard has taken your sister home. She thought that the fresh air would do her good.' Suddenly, he noticed her companions, and at once his face was wreathed in smiles as he grasped his brother's hand. 'Nick, my dear fellow! I had no idea you were back from the Continent! I'm very glad to see you!' Now that they were closer together, the likeness was most marked, especially since each face was reflecting the delight of the other. The very likeness, however, made the difference between the two starkly apparent, the pale dissipation of the one in sharp contrast to the healthy ruddiness of the other, so that they could more easily have been thought to be father and son, rather than older and younger brother.

'You will have to admit now that you were wrong, my Lord,' said Fliss. 'There is a member of your family who is glad to see you.'

'Ah, but you see, he suspects that I might have some money,' replied Lord Nick in a confidential tone. 'Later, he will try and touch me for a monkey!' At this point, Mrs Salisbury approached them and greeted Lord Nick with slightly guarded pleasure.

'Your servant, Elvira!' he declared, bowing with a flourish. Then he went on, 'What's the matter? Afraid of what I might do? Not here, surely! Anyway, I'm on my best behaviour. May I come to dinner?'

'Wait until you are asked,' she responded

94

tartly. Then, her expression softening, she went on, 'You are all welcome to dine with us a week tonight, if you should be free.' All the gentlemen accepted with pleasure, and soon afterwards Mrs Salisbury expressed a desire to leave.

Fliss agreed readily, saying, 'Yes indeed, ma'am. Melissa felt unwell, and has already gone with Richard, our brother who has just arrived with Lord Octavius.'

'Then you must be anxious to see how she does,' said Mrs Salisbury. They bade the gentlemen goodbye. Lord Octavius responded with his usual courtesy, and Sir James with rather less than his usual warmth.

'I trust that your sister will soon be well, and I look forward to meeting her in the future,' said Lord Nick with careless grace that just kept the right side of insolence.

As they were walking along Stall Street, Mrs Salisbury said thoughtfully and with some diffidence, 'I know you will forgive me for speaking to you on this matter for, although you are a grown woman, you have not had a great deal of experience. Lord Nick is . . . can be . . . very fascinating, but it might be as well to be a little cautious there. You must, of course, acknowledge him now that you have met him, but it would be wise to keep such an acquaintance to the minimum.'

'Why is that, ma'am?' asked Fliss, although she had guessed the answer anyway.

'I am afraid that his reputation is very bad,' replied her companion. 'In fact, to be blunt, he is a notorious rake. To be seen too much in his company would do neither you nor Melissa any good at all.'

'It will be difficult to avoid him altogether,' said Fliss thoughtfully. 'After all, he is James's friend.'

'Gentlemen, my dear, number a good many people among their acquaintance, whom they would not, or should not, present to ladies. And indeed, James himself—' She broke off suddenly, then resumed almost immediately in a much more lively tone, 'Oh look in that window! What a charming shade of ribbon! I do hope that they have enough of it to trim that bonnet of mine!' Fliss's interest was caught by her companion's obvious desire to change the subject, and she would have liked to have brought up the matter again when they came out of the shop. She wanted to know what it was that Mrs Salisbury had been about to say about James, but she did not know how to raise the topic without seeming over-curious.

There was also upon her mind the incident of Melissa's being suddenly overcome by faintness in the Pump Room. It had occurred immediately after they had caught sight of Richard and Lord Octavius and she could not escape the conclusion that Melissa must have been far more captivated by Octavius than she had seemed to be. It could be the case that the young naval officer was similarly smitten and, in a world where romance was everything, that would be entirely satisfactory. Unfortunately, the same objection that applied in Richard and Alice's case would also apply to any union between Melissa and Octavius. Neither the Bonsors, nor the Wintershills had a feather to fly with. At least, however, she did not have to worry now about whether to send a message home concerning Richard. Nor did she feel obliged to notify Alice of his presence in Bath. She would find that out for herself soon enough. Another blessing was that if Melissa was already smitten with Octavius, it was most unlikely that she would fall victim to the practised charms of Lord Nick. As she recalled to mind the member of the Bonsor family whom she had met most recently, she ventured to put to her hostess a question that was puzzling her.

'If Lord Nicholas is such a rake, why did you invite him to dine?'

Mrs Salisbury looked a little sheepish. 'I have to admit that I have a soft spot for a rogue,' she confessed. 'But for goodness sake, do not tell him so!' As Fliss remembered the coaxing way in which he had sought the invitation, she thought that Lord Nick had probably guessed.

They arrived in Laura Place to find Richard sitting with Melissa. 'How are you, my dear?'

97

asked Mrs Salisbury concernedly. 'I was truly shocked when I heard that you had fainted. I trust you are feeling better. Never say that you walked all the way back!' Melissa smiled and Fliss was pleased to see that her natural colour had returned and that she looked much more herself.

'I did not faint,' she said calmly. 'I was simply overcome for a moment, because it was crowded and rather warm. Yes, I did walk home, but Richard was with me, and I promise you that it was the best thing for me to do, for I felt much better once I was in the fresh air.'

'I am very glad you feel better, Lissa,' said Fliss. 'In all this agitation, though, I think that we have been so rude as to forget to present our brother to Mrs Salisbury!'

Their hostess brushed this aside easily. 'It is not surprising that you forgot under such circumstances,' she said smilingly. 'I am very pleased to meet you, sir. Where are you staying in Bath?'

'At the Pelican at present, with Octavius Bonsor, ma'am.'

'I have just met Lord Octavius in the Pump Room, and have invited him and his brother Lord Nick to dine with us next week. Perhaps you would like to join us?'

'Thank you, ma'am, I would be delighted to join you,' he replied. Fliss glanced at Melissa and saw that she had coloured up a little at the mention of Octavius Bonsor.

Later, after Richard had left, and Melissa had been persuaded to go up to her room to rest, Mrs Salisbury said to Fliss, 'That is going to give us quite an unusual problem. Because your brother and his friend are dining with us we shall be four men and three ladies. Now who shall we invite to make up the number of ladies?'

'What about Mrs Foreshore?' suggested Fliss mischievously. 'We might run out of things to say, but she will never let us down!'

'Wicked girl!' exclaimed her hostess smiling. 'Ah well, there is plenty of time. I shall think of someone.'

Meanwhile, their days always seemed to be full, not of household cares, as would have been the case at home, but of visits to the Pump Room, concerts, dances, and once, a visit to the theatre. Often, the group had the same composition: Fliss, Melissa, Mrs Salisbury, James, Lord Nick and Octavius. Occasionally, Richard joined them, but he was more often to be found amongst the group that surrounded Lady Susan Tryon and her daughter. Lord Nick spent the majority of his time flirting outrageously with all the ladies in turn, and particularly with Fliss, for whom he seemed to save his greatest absurdities. Fliss, remembering Mrs Salisbury's warning, was amused but not in the slightest danger of succumbing to his undoubted charm. As Nick's spirits rose, however, it seemed as if James became more and more morose, until eventually, halfway through the week, he came to call on the ladies in Laura Place.

'I am returning home today,' he said unsmilingly. 'There are one or two matters of business which I must not neglect. I have merely come to discover whether you, ma'am,'—and here he turned to Fliss—'have any messages to entrust to me.' Fliss was so overcome by the fact that he had called her 'ma'am' when he had been calling her by her first name that she could not think of anything to say.

'You are leaving Bath?' exclaimed his aunt. 'Surely you are not intending to miss my dinner?' James made an impatient sound.

'I beg that you will hold me excused,' he said stiffly.

'By no means,' replied Mrs Salisbury, drawing herself to her full height, and addressing him as if she were an aunt twenty years his senior. 'I will put it off for a few days, but I expect you to be there.'

He bowed, and would have withdrawn, but Fliss said, 'Pray send Mama and Papa and the children my best love.'

He turned back, his expression softening. 'Your servant, ma'am,' he replied, taking her hand and kissing it.

'It is just as well he is to be gone for a few days,' said his aunt after he had left. 'Perhaps he will come back in a better temper.' Fliss smiled uncertainly. She could not help wondering whether he was returning home because he wanted to see Mrs Grantham.

Exactly a week later, her speculations appeared to have been confirmed. One afternoon, when Mrs Salisbury was upstairs and Fliss was alone in the drawing-room, there was a knock at the front door. Shortly afterwards, Yare opened the door to admit Sir James accompanied by Mrs Grantham. Fliss looked at her in surprise, but Mrs Grantham hurried over and said, 'My dear, I made up my mind! James told me of all the fun that you were having here and I couldn't resist! I am putting up at the Christopher and I have come to join you!'

CHAPTER NINE

Mrs Grantham had never been anything other than courteous to Fliss. She had been more; she had been cordial. Fliss therefore found it hard to account for the fact that at the sight of the widow, her first feeling was one of consternation, to be followed immediately afterwards by annoyance. Fortunately, Mrs Grantham's enthusiasm was enough for two and by the time greetings had been exchanged, Fliss had regained control of herself.

'Is my aunt at home?' asked Sir James.

'Yes, but I think that she is resting,' replied Fliss.

'Then perhaps you will crave her kindness on Amanda's behalf,' he went on. 'I believe that she has rearranged her dinner for tomorrow night, and I was wondering whether she might allow Amanda to join the party.'

'James, I am sure I should not,' protested Mrs Grantham. 'After all, I have not met your aunt.'

'I am sure that she would be agreeable,' said Fliss, knowing her duty. 'She was only saying yesterday that she would still like to have another lady at table.'

'Then it is settled,' said James, smiling more broadly than Fliss thought was strictly necessary.

'By no means,' contradicted Mrs Grantham. 'I am not so discourteous as to accept an invitation that my hostess has not sanctioned. Mrs Salisbury might have issued another invitation unknown to Miss Wintershill. I will not impose upon her unless I have confirmation from her that my attendance is welcome.' Fliss could not help feeling pleased that Mrs Grantham should be so punctilious and she promised to speak to Mrs Salisbury as soon as she came downstairs. The visitors left soon afterwards and, looking out of the window, Fliss saw them walking down the street with Mrs Grantham leaning on Sir James's arm in what seemed to be a rather ostentatiously possessive way.

'So Mrs Grantham is staying at the Christopher,' was Mrs Salisbury's comment when she heard the news. 'She certainly did not wait long before coming here, did she?' Fliss made no comment. Clearly she and her hostess were thinking much the same thing about Mrs Grantham and Sir James.

That evening, they all attended a concert in the Lower Rooms and Fliss observed her brother in company with Miss Tryon. Neither one behaved indecorously, but to Fliss their regard for one another was quite plain. Her heart went out to them, but she could not consider their chances of happiness with any optimism. She turned and saw that Sir James had joined her. This evening he was dressed in dull gold velvet with a cream waistcoat embroidered with multi-coloured birds.

'Good evening, Felicity,' he said, looking admiringly at her gown of gold silk with a cream underdress. 'We match, I see.' He noticed the direction of her gaze and said quietly, 'Your brother is aiming a little high there, I think.'

'Yes, I know,' she agreed anxiously. 'But how can I tell him so without hurting him?' Suddenly she realized that she had accepted automatically his understanding of the situation, and furthermore that he could be trusted to keep quiet about it.

As if guessing her thoughts, he said, 'Don't

worry. I'm very discreet.'

Fliss sighed. 'I just hope that Richard will be so too,' she said. 'If only I could believe that this will die a natural death!'

'Richard is no boy in love for the first time,' James reminded her. 'He is a grown man, and I think that you should prepare yourself for a lasting attachment.'

They were silent for a time. Then Fliss said, 'Did you manage to settle your business matter satisfactorily?'

He looked at her blankly for a moment. 'My business matter?' Then he recollected himself and went on hastily, 'Oh yes, yes, that was easily dealt with.' Fliss decided that she had been right in her suspicions. He had had no real reason to go back to Roache Hall, apart from wanting to see Mrs Grantham.

With this in her mind, she said, 'Is Mrs Grantham coming tonight?'

'I believe not,' he replied, not sounding noticeably dashed. 'Shall we sit down?' More relieved about Mrs Grantham's absence than was really logical, Fliss allowed Sir James to find places for them. They were about to sit down when Lord Nick approached, looking dashing in dark blue with a waistcoat of a lighter shade.

'Miss Wintershill, your servant,' he drawled, bowing with careless grace. 'James, my dear fellow! May I join you, or shall I be interrupting a *tête-à-tête*?' Fliss coloured and glanced up at James's face. He did not look particularly pleased, and Fliss wondered whether he was annoyed at being coupled with her when his desires were set upon Mrs Grantham.

'By no means,' she said quickly. 'You are most welcome, Lord Nick.'

'Are you sure?' he asked mischievously. 'James does not look very approving.'

'Don't be absurd, Nick,' replied Sir James with a laugh that did not quite meet his eyes. 'It is as Felicity says; you are welcome to join us.'

'Splendid!' said Nick sitting down. 'We'll be quite a family party. Look, Tavy and Miss Melissa are coming to join us.' There's another hopeless romance, Fliss thought to herself looking at her sister and Lord Octavius before settling down to enjoy the music. During a break in the proceedings, Fliss had an opportunity to speak to both Alice and Richard. Alice came up to her first.

'I did not need to trouble you after all,' she said. 'I should have thought of applying to Uncle Tavy, but it did not occur to me.'

'Does your mother know of your attachment?' asked Fliss. She knew the answer before Alice said a word.

'No, I dare not tell her. I cannot imagine what we are going to do. Money is nothing to me, but to Mama it is everything; only I cannot give him up! I cannot!' There was such anguish in her voice and on her face that Fliss was glad that her back was turned to the assembled company.

Moments later, after Alice had returned to her mother's side, Richard crossed the room to speak to his sister.

'Isn't she an angel?' he said rapturously. 'Isn't she everything I said she was?'

'She seems very amiable,' replied Fliss honestly.

'Amiable? I should say so.' They were looking across at Alice, and at that moment Lady Susan stepped into their line of vision. Richard's expression changed to one very similar to that which had adorned Alice's features only moments before. 'Oh Fliss, what am I to do?' he asked her. Shortly afterwards it was time for them to resume their seats and James came back to sit with her. He looked rather annoyed.

Fliss ventured to say, 'Sir, your brow is very black! I trust I have done nothing to vex you?' He looked at her, his brow relaxed, and he smiled.

'No, you have done nothing wrong. It is the actions of others in imposing upon you that vex me.'

'Imposing?' she asked, mystified. 'But no one is imposing upon me, I think. Whom can you mean, sir?' Later, she was to wonder whether he meant that Lord Nick might be deceiving her with his nonsense.

'How many times do I have to tell you that my name is James?' he replied, not answering her question. 'But tell me, have you settled down well with my aunt?'

Fliss smiled. 'Oh, very well indeed! She has made us so welcome. I feel so spoiled, for I have nothing to do!' The musicians were by now clearly about to begin again, so there was no time to ask Sir James to repeat the remark that he had made immediately afterwards. It had sounded like 'high time'.

After the concert was over, as they were getting ready to leave, Octavius approached them.

'Alice and I have been talking about exploring some of the surrounding countryside,' he said. 'We were wondering whether you would all like to join us for a riding expedition on a day convenient to us all?'

Lord Nick accepted immediately. 'I have no engagements so any day will do for me. It would be too bad if we did not take advantage of this unexpected family gathering,' he replied. 'I shall feel quite patriarchal.'

'Impossible!' declared Octavius. 'You needn't pull rank on me. You're only my brother after all. So you can be fraternal if you like, or even avuncular for Alice's benefit, but you cannot possibly be patriarchal.'

'See what little respect my family has for me!' Nick declared mournfully to the rest of

107

the company. 'Is it any wonder that I fled for the Continent?'

'The wonder will be if we put up with your histrionics for more than ten minutes,' declared James sardonically. 'Have you ever thought of going on the stage, Nick?'

'Alas, no,' was the reply. 'I fear that the late hours would be injurious to my health.' There was a smothered giggle from Melissa. 'I see there is someone here who appreciates me,' he murmured with a grin.

'We will more of us appreciate you if you will just be quiet for the space of half-a-dozen sentences,' said James with a twinkle, before turning to Octavius. 'For my part I should be glad of a ride. How about next Wednesday? What do you say, ladies?'

Fliss looked a little doubtful. 'I am certainly free on Wednesday, but I have not ridden for some time,' she said.

'Then I will make sure that you have a very amenable mount,' smiled Octavius.

'You may safely leave the procuring of mounts for Felicity and Miss Melissa to me,' said Sir James masterfully. 'At what hour do you wish to set out?'

'At ten o'clock if that is agreeable. Richard and I are now staying at Nick's lodging, so we will come to you in Laura Place. But we will all meet again tomorrow at Mrs Salisbury's for dinner, will we not?'

The following evening, Fliss dressed with

particular care. Had she been accused of not wanting to be outdone by Mrs Grantham, she would have vigorously denied it, but she wanted to prove that a country girl could have some style about her. She was wearing the primrose evening gown that had arrived from the dressmaker and she had to acknowledge herself very well satisfied with the result. In addition, Mrs Salisbury's hairdresser had visited only that morning, and had cut and coaxed her heavy dark hair into a more becoming style, taking some away from her brow so that it did not seem to weigh her down so much, and the shape of her face was revealed more flatteringly. The last thing that she did was to clasp around her neck the diamond pendant that had been redeemed for her by Sir James. She put up her hand to her throat to touch it briefly, then she went to the communicating door and tapped on it.

Melissa had clearly gone to a good deal of trouble as well. Her blonde hair, more manageable than Fliss's, had been brushed till it shone and her white muslin gown made her look almost ethereal. Fliss could not help wondering if Lord Octavius would be impressed.

Certainly, when he arrived that evening with his brother and Richard he looked very appreciative, although Fliss, who was watching him carefully, could not detect any special attachment, as Melissa blushed and curtsied.

Lord Nick said, 'How comes it about that two ladies as lovely as yourselves have not been snapped up? Are all the men in Somersetshire blockheads?'

Melissa smiled uncertainly, then turned away, leaving Fliss to say, 'Not at all. I was engaged to be married a few years ago, but my fiancé died.'

'I'm sorry to hear it,' he replied, the mask of social assurance slipping briefly to reveal an expression of real regret. Then he carried on in his usual languid style. 'And your sister? She's much too beautiful not to be spoken for. Perhaps there's a squire or farmer languishing in her absence?'

'I shan't give away my sister's secrets, my Lord,' she answered smiling. Melissa, away from Lord Nick's disturbing innuendoes, was now talking and laughing easily with Octavius Bonsor.

'You probably don't know them all,' he said with a roguish grin. At that moment, Sir James came in with Mrs Grantham, who was looking extremely elegant in a gown of olive-green silk which admirably complemented her auburn hair. She was also wearing a magnificent emerald necklace. Fliss fingered her pendant again, more thankful than ever that it had not found its way around Mrs Grantham's neck.

'My dear Miss Wintershill!' she exclaimed as they came over to her. 'How charming you are looking! Do you not think so, James?'

James took Fliss's hand and kissed it, sending a frisson of awareness all the way up her arm.

'Certainly not,' he replied smiling down at Fliss. 'Charming is not an adequate description at all. I like the new hairstyle, by the way.'

'Yes indeed; very becoming,' agreed Mrs Grantham. 'I was just saying earlier that . . .' She broke off, then exclaimed, 'Good heavens! If it isn't Nick Bonsor! What unlucky chance has brought you here among these charming young ladies?' Lord Nick grinned and bowed with careless grace.

'Amanda Grantham, as I live and breathe! You behold me the picture of innocence! I am here merely in the guise of an older relative. That young fellow over there is my baby brother, to whom I'll present you, as long as you guarantee not to sully his youthful ears with tales of my scandalous past!'

'Past, my dear fellow?' murmured Sir James, one eyebrow raised. The two men laughed and for an instant, there was something in their stance and expression that made them look strangely alike. Lord Nick had chosen to wear purple, with a lighter coloured waistcoat embroidered in silver, and James was wearing a russet-coloured coat with a bronze waistcoat. In contrast to Nick, his complexion had a healthy tan, and he seemed to Fliss to be just as much at home here in a fashionable drawing-room as he did striding across the fields near Roache Hall.

'Pray excuse us for a while,' said Mrs Grantham, tucking her hand into the rake's arm. 'I want Nick to tell me all his wicked secrets!'

'How much time do you have?' asked Nick as they strolled away.

If Sir James was annoyed at the appropriation of the lady whom he had brought that evening then he did not show it, but turned to Fliss saying, 'I have made enquiries about a horse for you, and I believe that there will be no difficulty in procuring a suitable mount.'

'Thank you,' replied Fliss. 'You are very good.'

'Nonsense,' he said a trifle roughly. 'If I'd been very good, I'd have thought about that long ago, and enabled you to ride more at home. You could easily have ridden one of the horses at Roache Hall.'

'How kind of you to think of it!' exclaimed Fliss. 'But how eccentric of you to have kept all these extra horses stabled at the Hall just for your own use, and how strange that I have never had an inkling of their presence!'

He flushed a little. 'I always keep a horse for William,' he said defensively. There was no time to say more on this head, for Yare came in to announce dinner. Nevertheless, Fliss was touched by his kindness and kept thinking about it again during the evening.

At dinner, Fliss found herself seated with

112

Nick on one side of her and Richard on the other. Nick was an amusing table companion, keeping Fliss laughing with a stream of nonsense. For all that, she did not lose sight of Melissa sitting next to Octavius and giving him her full attention. She could also see out of the corner of her eye that Mrs Grantham was putting forth her best efforts in amusing James, and that he was responding with smiles and occasional laughter.

Richard, too, seemed determined to put his worries about Alice behind him, and enjoy the evening. All in all, thought Fliss, it would be perfect if only . . . but she could not think what the 'if only' might be. After the dinner was over, the ladies left the gentlemen to their wine.

'If Nick has anything to do with it, they'll be there for hours,' said Mrs Grantham dispassionately. But either Nick's counsels did not prevail, or else he had decided to abandon his customary habits, for a very short time later the door opened and Nick was one of the first, wandering casually over to where Melissa was playing the piano and singing. 'I am so pleased that I have come to Bath,' went on Mrs Grantham. 'There is so much to do; shopping, going to the Pump Room, meeting one's friends. I am told that there are some fine bursts of countryside around here. Do you ever go riding, Miss Wintershill?'

'As a matter of fact, some of us are to go in a

few days' time,' said Fliss.

'How delightful,' she replied. Only the rudest of people could have denied her an invitation. Fliss, while wishing that she was the rudest person, could not bring herself to achieve her desire.

'You are very welcome to come,' said Fliss. 'It is just a party of friends; mostly those you see now.'

'I should like it of all things,' said Mrs Grantham warmly. 'I am sure that James will procure me a mount. He is so obliging.'

'Yes, isn't he?' murmured Fliss.

Four days later, Sir James and Mrs Grantham arrived promptly at Laura Place, the lady looking dashing in a riding habit of olive green. Until her arrival, Fliss had been very pleased with the peat-brown habit which had belonged to Mrs Salisbury's daughter and which had been skilfully altered by Simpson. After the widow's appearance, she suddenly felt a little dowdy and underdressed. Melissa looked enchanting in a royal blue habit which she had had for her coming-out two years before and which Simpson had tweaked to give it a more fashionable touch. Alice, in a lighter shade of the same colour, was very pretty and it did not surprise Fliss at all that Richard was captivated with her. Her only anxiety would be to see that he did not spend his whole time in Alice's pocket and that Melissa did not do the same with Octavius.

Fliss was above all a country girl, and it was not until they were out of the city that she realized how much she had missed the open spaces, trees and hedgerows. She turned a glowing face to Sir James and when he smiled back at her she suddenly felt her heart skip a beat. He had found her a docile mount as promised and she soon found old skills returning and she began to relax. Moreover, she had every confidence in Sir James, who was a fine horseman, and on the alert for any difficulty that she might have.

As they set out, Octavius and Mrs Grantham led the way with Melissa riding beside her brother and Alice beside Lord Nick, and Fliss and James bringing up the rear. Once out in the countryside, the party sorted itself out a little and eventually Fliss found herself riding for a time next to Lord Nick whilst Sir James talked with Mrs Grantham, and the others rode together in a group.

'For a woman who says she cannot ride, you are doing remarkably well,' said Lord Nick, looking at her measuringly from beneath his rather heavy, lazy lids.

'I did not say I could not, I said it had been a long time, and so it has. And I have to admit, my Lord, that I am enjoying it very much indeed.'

'Oh why so formal?' he exclaimed. 'Please call me Nick.'

'I couldn't possibly,' she returned.

'I don't see why not. You call James by his Christian name.' When she hesitated, he went on, 'Perhaps you feel that to call me by my given name might not accord with the high respect in which you hold me. Now James, as we know, is such a frippery fellow—'

'Not at all,' she interrupted, laughing. 'It is simply that I have known James for a number of years. You, on the other hand, I only met a few days ago.'

'But does long acquaintance necessarily bring with it a desire for intimacy? I can think of people whom I have known for years with whom I have no wish to be more closely acquainted. Take my sister, for example!'

'Lord Nick, for shame!' exclaimed Fliss, laughing again almost in spite of herself.

'On other occasions, however, one need only know someone for an instant and immediately one desires intimacy with them.' He put one hand on his heart and cast her a look that was so exaggeratedly arch that she could not help but laugh once more.

'Yes, my dear sir, that is very true,' she acknowledged when she had finished laughing. 'But both you and I know that such is not the case here. I may have lived all my life in the country, and I may find you entertaining, but that does not make me as naïve as a farmyard hen.' It was Lord Nick's turn to burst out laughing.

'Very well, ma'am,' he said in much more

normal tones. 'I take your point. But I still maintain that sometimes a man can meet a woman, and he knows that she is special to him straight away. If you asked him to tell you why, he might not be able to give you a reason such as her beauty or her personality or her bewitching smile, although she might possess any of those. Perhaps in an effort to put her out of his mind, he pursues every woman under the sun, but none of them will do. The feeling will not be denied.' He was looking straight ahead of him, his expression very serious.

'I suppose it might be true,' she said after a moment's thought. 'I notice that you speak only for men, but I think that women also can feel such emotions. Your observations should not be limited to the sphere of romantic love. Friendships, for example, can be forged at a single meeting.'

'I would not dream of contradicting you, Miss Wintershill.' They rode on in silence for a short time, then Fliss asked a question which had been on her mind for some little time.

'For how long have you known James?'

'Oh, for nearly thirty years. We met at Eton and were friends from the first, thus bearing out the truth of your observation.'

'I could guess that you were close friends by the way in which you greeted one another,' said Fliss carefully, hoping to find out more and yet not wanting to seem as if she was prying.

'Closer at one time than we are now,' replied Lord Nick. 'I've been out of the country for two years and long before that, James had largely withdrawn from the London scene.'

'I've never been to London,' said Fliss, unaware of how wistful she sounded.

'Perhaps James will take you there one day,' murmured Nick provocatively.

'Why should he do that?' she asked defensively, blushing.

'I'm sure he'll think of a reason; another aunt for you to visit, perhaps? Shall we ride on and join the children?' As Fliss could not think of a reply to this outrageous speech, she was very glad to do as he suggested, thinking that it might be as well to rearrange the party a little, anyway. Richard was spending rather too much time with Alice, and Melissa had not left Lord Octavius's side since they had got out of the city.

In fact, Richard and Alice had been making the most of the opportunity of talking together uninterrupted.

'When do you think I can approach your mother?' asked Richard urgently, and not for the first time.

'Oh Richard, I don't know,' answered Alice, her anxiety communicating itself to her mount, who shied a little. 'I have tried to hint to her that I am not inclined towards Mr Paranforth, or indeed towards any marriage arranged for mercenary reasons, but she seems quite deaf to anything that I might say.'

'Mr Paranforth!' exclaimed Richard. 'Is it certain then that he is coming to Bath to offer for you?'

'Nothing is certain,' replied Alice wretchedly, 'but I fear that it must be so. We were quite happily settled in London, and I cannot think of any other reason why Mama would suddenly want us to come here, for neither of us is ill and needing to drink that dreadful water.'

'But one good thing has resulted from it: we are able to meet one another,' said Richard smiling at her.

'As if I would deny that,' returned Alice, answering him with a smile as loving as his own.

'Then let me speak to your mother,' urged Richard. 'I so much want to claim you before the world with an honourable engagement.'

'There is nothing I want more,' confessed Alice. 'But you don't know Mama as I do. If I venture to be more assertive, she just says that I'm too young to know my own mind. But I'm not, Richard!'

'I know that, sweet,' he answered. He thought for a moment then went on, 'Do you think that your uncle might stand our friend?'

'Tavy?' exclaimed Alice, puzzled.

'No, not Octavius,' replied Richard. 'I was

119

thinking of Lord Nick. It's just that Tavy and I are now sharing his lodging, and I get on pretty well with him. He is closer to your mother in age, and I was wondering whether he might be prepared to help us?' Alice looked doubtful.

'I suppose he might, although I have to say that I hardly know him. He's been abroad, and then, of course, I was away at my seminary and he was mostly in London. But Richard, I doubt whether Mama would listen to him. She talks about him as a libertine and a blot on the family escutcheon. I doubt whether his word would influence her at all.'

Richard sighed. 'I wish I knew how to convince her that I would be an acceptable suitor for your hand,' he said. 'God knows we'd have little enough if we married, but that little would all be yours.'

'Don't say "if" Richard, say "when",' insisted Alice. 'We will manage it somehow. Otherwise, what is the alternative? Could you bear to see me married to Mr Paranforth, or some other wealthy man of Mama's choosing?' Richard's hands tightened involuntarily on his rein and his horse reacted nervously.

'I would sooner kill him,' he vowed.

'Oh pray do not talk so violently!' cried Alice.

'Forgive me! I am allowing my imagination to run away with me. Let us not spoil the time that we have. Whatever happens, I promise that we will be together somehow. Hush now, though. My sister and your uncle are catching up with us.'

For a time, the party rode on as a close group, with the conversation being very general and somewhat disconnected. Soon afterwards, they turned back for home, and on their return, Fliss found herself riding with James, whilst a little ahead of them, Mrs Grantham and Lord Nick rode together flirting desperately.

'Having brought you to Bath, I feel in some way responsible for you,' said James, 'so perhaps I should have warned you before now that Nick is a notorious rake.'

'First Mrs Salisbury warned me, and now you,' said Fliss good-humouredly. 'How naïve do you think I am, James? I was certainly able to discern that for myself.'

'In that case, I have to say that I'm surprised that you were prepared to flirt with him so enthusiastically,' he retorted.

'You must have uncommon powers of hearing and discernment, James, if you think that you were able to detect a flirtation taking place all of twenty yards away,' she said tartly.

'Felicity . . .'

'Furthermore, I cannot help but pity Mrs Grantham if you were riding next to her with half your attention fixed upon two other people. You are not very gallant, sir.'

'Felicity, I make every allowance for your intelligence,' persisted James, speaking a little louder and with a little less patience, 'but you are wholly lacking in any experience of dealing with such a man.'

'Oh for goodness' sake, James, what do you think could possibly happen here, amongst friends, on horseback?' she said exasperatedly.

'I am not simply referring to today,' he said impatiently. 'You are being unconscionably foolish if you think that riding with him safely in company means that all danger is past. Nick, to put it bluntly, is a practised seducer of anything in petticoats! No doubt after your protracted flirtation with him today, he regards you as fair game!'

Fliss coloured, as much with anger as with embarrassment. 'Well, I suppose you must know, intimate with him as you are!' she retorted swiftly.

'And what is that supposed to mean?' he asked slowly and with a hint of menace.

'I merely wondered how you could consider yourself to be a friend of such a "practised seducer" unless . . .' Her voice faded away. Suddenly, she realized that she had gone too far.

'Unless . . . ?' he prompted.

'It was nothing,' she said quickly. Just a passing thought.'

'Unless I am one myself, I think you were going to say,' he said silkily.

'No . . . no, of course not, I . . .'

'Felicity my dear, I really think that you

believe you can take charge of such as Nick in the same way that you control the children of your household. It is high time that you learned you are mistaken.'

'What do you mean?' she asked suspiciously.

'Simply this: tomorrow, I'm taking you for a drive—should you chance to be free, of course.'

'Yes, I am free, but James—'

'Don't argue. I am taking you for a drive and you will learn, my dear Felicity, how a rake behaves.'

'This is preposterous! I won't do it! And if you think you can order me about like this . . .'

'I'm not ordering you. I asked you if you were free, and you told me that you were. I'll collect you at ten o'clock, and we will play a little game. You can be Miss Wintershill, a young lady from the country, and I will be Sir James Singleton, a gentleman whom you think you know.'

CHAPTER TEN

The day dawned bright and clear for James and Fliss's outing as Sir James Singleton and Miss Wintershill. Fliss had been more disturbed by her conversation with him than she was prepared to admit, even to herself. It was as if she had caught a glimpse of an entirely different man from the one she had known for ten years. The night before their outing, she found it hard to sleep, wondering what exactly he might be planning. She had half a mind to tell him that she would not go, but then he might think that she was afraid and that would never do!

She was glad to escape having to discuss the matter with Melissa, for her sister had gone out earlier that morning to spend some time with Ruth Stringer. Fliss had greeted this news with some surprise.

'Miss Stringer must certainly improve on acquaintance,' she had said in puzzled tones.

'Yes, I think she does,' Melissa had replied airily. 'Do you want anything in town, should I chance to go there?' Fliss did not want anything and she was glad to get away with saying nothing about her own outing. It only occurred to her later to wonder why she should be so embarrassed about going driving with someone whom she had known for nearly half her life.

Promptly at ten o'clock, Sir James arrived. Fliss was ready to go—had been ready for the past half-an-hour at least—but for some reason she felt it necessary to loiter in her room for a full quarter of an hour before going downstairs. She had taken particular care with her appearance and was glad that her new amber walking dress had arrived in time from the dressmaker. She was quite determined not to allow James to intimidate her. Who did he think he was, warning her about Lord Nick's intentions as if she were a parlour boarder in one of the seminaries in Queen's Square? Well, she would go, but he need not think that he would be able to play off any tricks on her!

For his part, James had been having second thoughts. His suggestion that he and Fliss go out for a drive together had been an impulse of the moment. Seeing her at ease with Nick had so infuriated him that he had only just managed to conquer his feelings sufficiently in order to converse with her, and her amused rejection of his warnings and advice had filled him with a desire to demonstrate to her in practical terms how very unsafe a rake could be. A time of quiet reflection had made him think again. He did not want to distress or frighten her; certainly he did not want to do anything that would turn her against him. Eventually, he decided to wait upon her in Laura Place as arranged, but he would behave towards her in the same way as he had always done. Then, when they were out of the city, he would tell her enough about his and Nick's past history to put her on her guard.

Such was still his resolve when Fliss entered the drawing-room where he was being entertained by his aunt. He arose at her entrance, smiled, bowed and presented her with a posy of flowers. She thanked him, and

Mrs Salisbury said, 'What a charming gesture! But then James is such a gentleman!'

'Yes, ma'am, I know,' replied Fliss.

'Have a lovely drive, and bring her back safely,' said Mrs Salisbury. Then she added, 'What a foolish thing to say! Of course you will!'

'I shall endeavour so to do,' replied James, bowing slightly. Glancing at Fliss, he saw that she was looking happy, confident and even a little smug, and suddenly he felt angry at her assumption that he was as harmless as his aunt's lap-dog. At once he renewed his vow to teach her a lesson. He smiled back at her, taking care that his expression was not in Mrs Salisbury's line of vision. This time his smile was subtly different, and he saw the look on her face change from one of confidence to one that was much more uncertain.

For her part, Fliss found that she was on the receiving end of the kind of measuring look that appeared to be assessing not simply the style and cut of her gown, but exactly what she might be wearing underneath it! Involuntarily, she took a step back and looked at him as she had found herself doing so recently with alarming frequency, noticing again his broad shoulders, upright figure and manly features. Small wonder that Mrs Grantham had chased him all the way to Bath! She could almost imagine doing the same herself! She blushed at her thoughts but thankfully, Sir James was at that moment bidding farewell to his aunt and repeating his promise to bring his passenger back safely. This comforted Fliss a little, but not very much. Suddenly she felt very unsure of him and of herself.

Outside the door, a barouche was waiting with two horses in harness and a driver on the box. Fliss had half expected Sir James to be driving himself. The fact that he was not doing so unnerved her even more, and she hesitated on the pavement.

James, noticing her uncertainty, murmured in a silky tone, 'Craven, Miss Wintershill? And so soon? We needn't go if your courage has failed you.'

'Certainly not,' replied Fliss squaring her shoulders. She took his hand in order to climb into the barouche and, as she did so, realized that that was exactly what he had intended. He climbed in beside her and signalled to the driver to start. She looked at him a little apprehensively, but he smiled in such a disarming way that she could not help smiling back and her fears were somewhat allayed. As they travelled through the city, he talked so amusingly and normally, drawing her attention to places and people that they passed on their journey, that she began to think that the whole enterprise had been just a joke that had long since run its course.

Eventually after a lull in the conversation Fliss ventured to say, 'Where are you taking me?'

'I was waiting to see when you would become curious enough to ask,' he replied. 'I wonder, shall I tell you?' There was a teasing, almost an arch note in his voice that suddenly made her decide to try playing him at his own game.

'I'm sure I do not care,' she replied, tossing her head and looking away from him. He laughed softly, and she turned back to face him in shock. For a brief moment, he had sounded exactly like Nick, and she had half expected to see that Sir James had suddenly turned into his rakish friend.

'How very convenient for me,' he murmured. 'Now I may take you anywhere I like. You have just given me permission to do so!'

Deciding that he needed no encouragement after all she said in her normal tone, 'Seriously, sir, where are we going?'

He leaned towards her. 'How much do you want to know?' he asked. 'Should I demand a "fee" of some sort, I wonder?' Fliss blushed and turned away. 'I wonder, have you any idea how adorable you look when you blush? So few women can do so nowadays.'

'Pray do not be absurd, Sir James,' she said, trying to sound normal even though her heart was starting to beat rather fast, partly from fear, and partly owing to some other emotion to which she dared not put a name.

'I hope you do not mean to ask me not to say what I think,' he said. 'If I find you adorable, can I not say so? As for our destination, you can see from yonder sign that we are leaving Bath by the Exeter road, and so your fears are allayed.'

They were anything but. Whilst they were in Bath itself, Fliss knew that James would keep within the bounds of propriety. Once they were unobserved, however, she was unsure of what this new, audacious James might do. It happened that the sign pointing to Exeter had been on her side of the carriage and he had leaned over a little to point it out to her. Now, he seemed to be sitting closer to her than before and was looking at her, a half smile playing about his lips. She became increasingly aware of the fact that he was bigger and stronger than she and that he had her completely in his power.

In order to divert his attention from herself and to the outing, she said quickly, 'How far were you intending to go?'

'As far as I can get away with,' he replied audaciously, and she gasped with shock.

'Sir James!' she exclaimed. 'I am astonished that you should say such a thing! Please, let us talk normally.'

'Why, what can you mean, Miss Wintershill?' he asked her, all bland innocence. 'I was simply stating my intentions of travelling as far as the day and weather will permit.' He paused briefly then went on, 'The coachman knows my intentions. He will follow my orders to the letter and will not turn round.' He paused again. 'Until I tell him, that is. If you will look over to your side of the carriage, my dear, you will see a fine burst of countryside.' Fliss turned to look, but when she turned back she found that Sir James had moved yet closer, and that it was impossible for her to lean back without allowing him to put his arm around her.

'Sir James, I think . . .' she began.

'Don't think, sweetheart,' he replied, leaning even closer to her so that they were touching. 'Just relax and enjoy yourself.'

'And what makes you think that I am enjoying this?' she asked him, shrinking back. She tried to sound indignant, but could not quite succeed in keeping the frightened tremble out of her voice.

'Did you not get into the carriage with me?' he answered. 'No lady gets into a carriage with Solitaire unless she wants to be alone with him.'

'Sir James, please,' she protested; then the arm that was resting behind her came around her shoulders and she was pulled into his arms.

'It's all right, sweet,' he murmured, looking down at her lazily. 'You don't need to ask; I know what you want.' She started to struggle in earnest, but her struggles seemed to affect him not at all. Carefully, he imprisoned her

130

one free arm with his left hand, and with his right lifted her chin.

'Sir James, no . . . I . . .'

'Stop all this foolish chatter,' he drawled. 'Your lips were meant for something far more agreeable.' She was very conscious of his strength, so much greater than hers. She was furiously angry at his manhandling of her, and his ruthless disregard for her feelings, but at the same time, there was something deep within her that held its breath as he made ready to kiss her. She closed her eyes, knowing herself powerless to break away. For a long moment nothing happened, then suddenly he kissed her briefly on the brow and she was free. She opened her eyes to find that he was sitting once more in his original place. 'Well, Felicity,' he said at last, 'how did you like being in the hands of a rake?'

She stared at him, unable to take in his sudden change of role, and half expected him to pounce upon her again at any moment. Then when he remained in his place, she began to realize what he had been doing.

'You were frightening me on purpose!' she exclaimed. He inclined his head, his face serious. 'Oh, James, how could you! And to think I really thought . . . believed for a moment that . . .' With an exasperated little sound, she turned away from him, her eyes fixed on the scenery, her mind in a turmoil.

He left her in quietness for a few moments,

then said gently, 'Felicity—I'm sorry.'

She did not answer him immediately, but after a few moments, she half turned her face towards him again, and said in hurt tones, 'How can you be sorry, when you frightened me quite deliberately? It was . . . unkind of you, James.'

'Yes, I know. I wanted to put you on your guard against the kind of man who might take advantage of you.'

Her anger flared up again, and she said swiftly, 'How dare you patronize me?'

'Such was not my intention, believe me,' he said sincerely, leaning towards her. 'I have the greatest respect for your intelligence. But even the most intelligent person, outside their normal sphere of activity, can easily be wrong-footed.' He paused, then, when she did not reply, he added tentatively, 'I've already apologized. I'll do so again if that will help.'

Her anger was beginning to give way to curiosity, and she remembered that she still knew next to nothing about his life in London, when he and Nick had been close friends. There would never be a better time to question him. But because she was still somewhat annoyed, she said, 'You were unfair to me.'

'Yes, I know,' he admitted.

'Did you really plan this yesterday?' she demanded. 'Because if you did, I think it must be the most conniving, sly thing I've ever heard, and I don't think I shall be able to forgive you.' He was silent for a moment.

'I would be less than honest if I said otherwise,' he said at last. 'After all, I told you what I planned to do right from the very beginning.'

'Yes, I know: I didn't expect you to be so good at it.'

He smiled humourlessly. 'Perhaps I should feel flattered,' he answered. He paused briefly, then went on, 'I want you to know that after I left you yesterday, I thought better of my decision. I came to Laura Place this morning with the intention of taking you for a perfectly ordinary, unalarming drive.'

Fliss looked at him. 'I see! So it is my fault, I suppose!' she said indignantly.

'Did I say that?' he asked her, in a tone almost as angry as her own. 'Look, there is an inn a little way along from here. Let's stop there for some refreshment. I promise you I'll keep in line. And I'll tell you something of my story. Perhaps then you might understand some of my reasons for acting the way I did.' Would she trust him? She looked straight at him, and his gaze held hers steadily. Then she smiled: it was a small, slightly strained expression, but at least she did smile.

'I am a little thirsty,' she admitted. He smiled back at her and suddenly everything seemed much more normal.

The inn where they stopped was very small,

but there were no other customers and the smiling landlady was very happy to serve them whilst they sat on the little bench outside.

'It wouldn't be fitting for you to sit in the tap-room,' said James. Fliss could not help wondering what Solitaire would have done. The baronet ordered ale for himself and lemonade for Fliss at her request. When they were both settled with their drinks, she sitting on the bench, he standing beside it, he said, 'I think that the best way to proceed will be if you ask me anything you wish to know. I promise you I'll answer truthfully unless it means betraying someone else's secrets. Will that be satisfactory for you?'

Fliss nodded. She took a sip of lemonade, then said, 'Tell me about your friendship with Lord Nick.'

He stiffened a little, and some of his easiness appeared to leave him. But he said good-humouredly enough, 'I expect you know by now that we were at school together. We were not exactly model pupils, and we got up to all kinds of larks. After that we went up to Cambridge and wasted a lot of time and money there, our own and other people's, before eventually getting ourselves sent down—I forget for what. Cambridge proving too hot for us, we went on to London and became men of the town. What next?'

'Why are you called Solitaire?' she asked, taking another mouthful of lemonade.

134

'Partly because of my name—Singleton— and partly, as Nick said, because of the single diamond that I habitually wore in my cravat. Partly . . .' He stopped and looked down, conscious of the need to measure his words.

Misunderstanding his silence, Fliss prompted him. 'Partly?' Still he said nothing so she went on, 'James, you promised me that you would answer truthfully, if you could. Are you perhaps afraid that you may compromise another person?'

'How easy it would be for me to say so,' he said ruefully. 'But it would not be the truth and I promised you that, did I not? What I have already told you is only half the truth, which will not do at all. I must go on, even though it may make you hate me.' He took a deep breath. 'Another reason is that . . . er . . . that young girls were strictly advised not to be alone with me.'

'I'm not surprised,' said Fliss a little tartly.

'I suppose I deserved that.' He paused. 'The last reason was that if I had a pistol in my hand, then one shot was always enough.'

'One shot!' exclaimed Fliss. 'Have you by any chance . . . duelled, sir?'

'I have been out four times. I'm not proud of it.'

'Did you . . . kill anyone?' ventured Fliss, almost in a whisper.

'Will you be disappointed if I say no?' he asked her a little cynically.

135

'Why should you suppose that I should be so bloodthirsty?' she asked him angrily. 'I should be glad if you had not been responsible for anyone's death.'

'Well I was not. But neither did I ever miss. Each time, I hit exactly where I intended to do so.'

'Why . . . why did you duel?' asked Fliss after a short time.

'I cannot tell you the details—and this time it is truly because of what I told you before, about being discreet concerning other people's affairs, but I can tell you . . . that they were all over a woman.'

'A woman?' murmured Fliss, thinking of Mrs Grantham, and trying not to be emotionally disturbed by something that had happened a dozen years before.

'Women, I should have said. Well, Felicity? Have you learned enough to satisfy you?'

'Not quite.' She paused. 'James—were you a rake?'

'My poor innocent,' he said mockingly, but Fliss got the feeling that he was mocking himself as much as he was her. 'Have you just managed to work that out? Let's have it all out now, shall we? Yes, I was a rake: I drank, I gambled, I womanized, I duelled.'

'In company with Nick?'

'Often, but not exclusively with Nick.' By now they had finished their refreshment and he went on in a different tone, 'Come now, it is time we returned. Are you ready?' She nodded, and he called for the horses to be put to. 'I'll tell you anything else you want to know on the way back,' he promised, whilst this was being done. They approached the barouche and he handed her in. It was only when she was seated beside him that she realized that she had got in with him without a trace of the apprehension that had filled her at the beginning of the outing, and this after the revelation that he had just made.

They travelled for a time in silence, then at last Fliss said, 'May I ask some more questions?'

He sighed. 'Have you not had enough sensations for today?' he asked, with a trace of bitterness.

'I'm not seeking after sensations,' she retorted indignantly. 'After all, you yourself said that I might ask. I merely wanted to understand you; to know why you are not . . . not . . .'

'Why Nick continues his ruinous career and why I have largely retired from London?' She nodded. 'Very well then, you had best prepare to hear my life history. I'm afraid it doesn't make for very edifying listening.

'After Nick and I had been sent down from Cambridge, we went to London where we began our careers, namely, making ourselves as notorious as possible. My father, seeing how things were going, decided that I needed steadying down so he set about arranging a marriage for me. I was then living on an allowance and my gambling, though prodigious, was not notable for its success. The lady picked out for me was four years older than myself, wealthy in her own right and disposed to be fond of me. I found myself backed into a corner and so I agreed. I was then twenty years of age.

'We remained in London after our marriage and soon my wife was with child. She was unwell throughout the pregnancy and did not survive the birth. I was left, just twenty-one, a widower with one child, whom you know—William, of course—and a huge fortune. Well, you can imagine how I carried on. Fortunately by that time I had learned to gamble rather better and the money did not disappear as quickly as it might have done. All the time my son was growing up. Almost in spite of myself, I began to take an interest in him as he grew.

'Nick was still my boon companion, but I had other friends, among them one Stephen Savage. He was older than me—probably about as old as I am now—and he had a son, Tony, who was about twenty. There was much the same age gap between Stephen and Tony as there was between William and myself. I watched them closely, and I admired them because there seemed to be a friendship between them that had been lacking between me and my father. I should tell you, I suppose, that when my marriage had no steadying effect upon me, my father was not afraid to show his extreme disapproval, and although there was never an estrangement between us, we were never really close. He died a few weeks after my wife, and I inherited the title from him, a house and land in London, and another huge fortune.

'Anyway, to resume, Stephen was a hell-raiser like Nick and me, and he treated his son as a roistering companion; more like a friend than a son, really. I remember thinking to myself, that's how I want it to be between William and me. Then one evening, Stephen was off with a ladybird of his choice and Tony went to a notorious gaming hell and dipped very deep. By the end of the evening, he'd gambled away everything he possessed and, because he and his father were so close, he'd managed to gamble away a large part of what Stephen possessed as well. That night, he went back to the lodgings which he and Stephen shared. Had Stephen come home it might have been different, but Stephen was still with his mistress at her house, so when Tony arrived home, he hanged himself.'

Fliss gasped. 'How horrible!' she exclaimed.

'Save your anguish, my dear. You've only heard the half of it. When Stephen discovered what had happened he sought out the man who had gambled with Tony that night and challenged him to a duel. When they fought, he deliberately laid himself open to his opponent's sword thrust and was killed outright. Nick was acting as his second and, on discovering Stephen's death, he took up his own sword, continued the fight on Stephen's behalf, and killed the other man. He was then forced to flee the country.

'I'd lost three friends, all within the space of a couple of nights. Furthermore, I'd lost my admiration of the way that Stephen and his son had lived. After Nick had left for the Continent I went home and looked at my son. I resolved that never if I could help it would I receive such news of him as Stephen had received concerning Tony. William was ten years old when I purchased Roache Hall and moved there with him and my household. You would then have been about fifteen and at school.'

There was a long silence after he had finished speaking. Eventually Fliss simply said, 'Do you ever miss London?'

'I wonder whether perhaps what you are really asking me is whether I miss my roistering life,' he answered. 'Well, the answer is, not really! With Nick gone, much of what we had done had lost its savour. Perhaps, too, I had been beginning to tire of the life anyway. So no, I don't miss it, but sometimes it catches up with me—witness Nick's advent, for example.'

'And Mrs Grantham?' ventured Fliss.

'Mrs Grantham was never a roistering companion of mine,' he answered, laughing a little. 'Whatever made you think of her?'

'I don't know,' said Fliss blushing. 'Oh look, we are coming back into Bath now.'

'Yes, but before this conversation is quite done, there is one more thing I must say: you accused me earlier of blaming you for my actions. Such was not my intention. But when you came downstairs looking as if you did not take my warnings seriously, I suddenly saw red. I'm sorry that I frightened you, but my actions, though misguided, were driven by real concern.' He paused briefly, then added, 'Forgive me?' She looked at him, and at once was reminded of his many kindnesses.

'Yes ... yes, of course,' she replied.

'Thank you,' he said quietly.

With their return to the busy streets the intimate nature of their conversation ceased and they returned to indifferent subjects. But Fliss, looking at his tanned, strong-looking face with its deep lines riven from nose to mouth, could not help thinking how little one could know of someone even though he might have been a part of one's life for a number of years.

On their arrival back at the house, James did not go in, saying that he had an appointment elsewhere. She was just thinking that she would be glad of a time of quiet reflection to go over all that she had heard and experienced that morning, when there was a knock at the door. Pausing in the hall, she turned to see Richard on the threshold looking the picture of anxiety. Thinking that he must have heard bad tidings from home she hurried towards him saying, 'What is it? What's wrong? Is it bad news?'

'The very worst,' he replied. 'Paranforth is in town.'

CHAPTER ELEVEN

Conscious of the need for discretion, Fliss hustled her brother into the bookroom which was downstairs and took off her bonnet and cloak.

'Now tell me what this is all about,' she said. 'From whom did you have this news? Is it certain?' Richard sat down, his head in his hands. 'Yes, it is quite certain,' he said despondently. 'He arrived this morning. There was a huge ring of bells, so Tavy and I went to find out who it was. He has his own coach, Fliss, as fine as anything I have seen! And he is staying in the York House in the very best suite.'

'Perhaps he is just here to drink the waters and take the bath,' suggested Fliss. Richard shook his head.

'No, for Tavy says that he overheard Alice's

mother telling Nick that at least Alice would be marrying money which would go to make up in some way for his profligacy. Oh Fliss, what are we to do?' Fliss looked at her beloved oldest brother. For as long as she could remember, her brothers and sisters had all come to her with their problems, and usually, she had been able to come up with a solution. This time, she could think of no answer.

'Have you been able to speak to Alice since this happened?' she asked him.

'No I haven't seen her, but you are right, Fliss, that is the next step. Whatever we do, we must agree upon.' He jumped up and gave her a quick hug. 'Thank you, Fliss! You always know what to do.' He left almost immediately. Fliss was left with the strange feeling that she had given some advice, but with the conviction that she was not entirely sure what that might be. Once up in her bedroom she knocked on Melissa's door but there was no answer. Melissa was obviously still out with Ruth Stringer.

Fliss sat down in one of the dainty chairs set beside the fireplace in order to think. She had to admit to herself that had Melissa been there, she would have found it difficult to share either of the matters which were uppermost in her mind. Richard had not given permission for her to speak about his affairs, so however much she might wish it, she could not confide in anyone. Even if she felt able to do so, Melissa would probably not have been her chosen confidante.

The truth was that her sister had been rather distant recently. Ruth Stringer had been taking up rather a lot of her time. Looking back, however, it seemed to Fliss that Melissa's rather distracted state dated from the reappearance of Octavius Bonsor. No, had she the choice she would probably confide in someone who had proved himself to have had a wide experience of the world—Sir James Singleton. She was certain that he would be discreet. After all, he had proved to be the soul of discretion concerning his own affairs.

That brought her neatly to the second of the two situations which demanded her consideration. She went over in her mind the events that had taken place during the drive that morning: his flirting, the way that he had drawn closer to her in the carriage, and the moment when he had nearly kissed her. She found herself wondering whether he had desisted out of respect for her, or because he had not really wanted to kiss her at all. From there it was only a small step to think about whether she had been disappointed that he had not done so, but the answer to this question was far too embarrassing to be dwelt upon.

It was not many days afterwards however, that she was to discover that however discreet Richard and Alice thought they were being, their romance was by no means a secret. She went to the Pump Room with Melissa and Mrs Salisbury. Melissa appeared preoccupied yet again, until she met up with Ruth Stringer, when suddenly she gained a good deal more animation.

'I thought that Melissa did not care for that young woman,' remarked Mrs Salisbury to Fliss.

'Yes, so did I,' Fliss replied. 'Perhaps, away from London, she is proving to be more agreeable.'

'Perhaps,' agreed Mrs Salisbury. Then she added in a diffident tone, 'I would not for the world appear to be over-critical of your sister, my dear, but I have to say that I feel she is rather neglecting you.' Fliss had been feeling much the same thing, but she did not want to seem disloyal by criticizing her sister to another. Before she could either protest or agree, however, Melissa and Ruth both came up to them.

'Oh, Miss Wintershill, will it be all right if Melissa and I go to the shops?' asked Ruth. 'I have a length of ribbon that I want to match.'

Fliss looked into the face of Ruth Stringer, and wondered why she could not like the girl when she was always perfectly amiable. After all, she could not help her rather pointed nose, thin lips, pale eyes and sandy brows. She felt a little better when, after she had agreed to the expedition and the girls had left, Mrs Salisbury turned to her and said, 'I know that the girl cannot help her looks, but I always feel that she could be very sly.' Perhaps it was that last word that Mrs Salisbury had used that made Fliss suddenly alert. At once, she scanned the Pump Room. Richard had just come in and indeed was exchanging a few words with Melissa and Ruth as they left. There was no sign of Octavius. Before she had time to think about what this might mean and what she ought to do about it, they had been approached by Mrs Foreshore.

'My dear Mrs Salisbury, you will be wondering where on earth I have been over the past few days and feeling neglected, I'm sure, except that I am certain that Miss Wintershill is not neglecting you, so if you have been neglected it has only been by me! Well, I have been to visit my niece in Bristol, and she has had such a pretty baby! A dear little girl, just like her mama, except that in certain lights she is like her papa, and at other times she looks like nobody in particular. How I do wish I could have brought a picture back to show you!'

'How pleased you . . .' began Mrs Salisbury, but Mrs Foreshore, needing no help whatsoever, took up her story again.

'Oh indeed I was! But you know, however welcoming other people may be, there is nowhere quite like one's own home is there? And indeed I am very glad to be back for I can see that a number of people have arrived in my absence.'

'Yes indeed,' began Fliss, intending to say that one of them was her brother. But Mrs Foreshore, having begun her performance as a monologue, had no intention of adding any other speaking parts at this stage.

'Mr Paranforth, for example! Now he is said to be a very warm man, and anyone can see that he has his heart set upon that pretty young granddaughter of the Duke of Brigham, and a fine match it will be for her if it comes about, because all the Bonsors are as poor as church mice, so that handsome young man can look as soulful as he likes, I do not think he will have any success! But I must not linger! I see Mrs Coot over there and I have not spoken to her for an age.'

'Lucky Mrs Coot,' murmured Sir James who had appeared during Mrs Foreshore's last speech. 'Or perhaps not so lucky. She could easily be there till midnight. I wonder, have there ever been cases of anyone actually expiring whilst she was talking to them?'

'James, really,' exclaimed his aunt, trying not to laugh.

'Yes, really,' he retorted. 'Does she ever stop, Elvira?'

'No, she just leaves,' admitted his aunt. 'Oh, will you excuse me? I see Maude Brankstone waving to me.' She moved away from them.

'For all that that woman is tedium

147

personified, she does notice a thing or two,' remarked Sir James. 'Have you warned Richard that he may be aiming too high?' Fliss looked up at him. His face was full of concerned interest, and suddenly the temptation to confide in him was too great to withstand.

'Oh James, I don't know what to do,' she sighed. 'He is quite determined, I think, but I cannot see that he has any hope of success—in pleasing her family, I mean.'

'From my observations I would say that his sentiments are returned,' he replied. 'But I do not know what good that will do either of them.' They were looking towards where Richard was talking to Alice and her mother. Lady Susan did not look to be particularly welcoming, and the conversation taking place between them seemed rather laboured. As they watched, the group was joined by Mrs Grantham and a gentleman whom Fliss did not recognize. She looked up at James questioningly. 'That's Paranforth,' he said, confirming her suspicions. 'I have not met him for a number of years, but I do recognize him.'

'He does not look at all well,' replied Fliss. 'I wonder whether he is here just for his health after all?'

The gentleman whom they were discussing was quite a portly man, only a little taller than Mrs Grantham herself, and with a pale complexion. Not by any means could he be described as a young girl's dream of romance. Fliss knew that she was naturally biased in Richard's favour, but it would be a very strange young woman indeed who, on appearance alone, could possibly prefer that sickly-looking middle-aged man to a fine young upstanding naval officer.

With Mr Paranforth's arrival, Lady Susan's manner underwent a marked change. She became more animated and her smiles were more forthcoming. Richard she totally ignored, managing in the way that only an experienced society woman can to elbow him almost entirely out of the group. Eventually Richard bowed and left, turning to approach Fliss and James. The working of his face showed that he was deeply moved.

'Fliss,' he said, his voice a little too loud for discretion. 'There's no bearing it!'

'No indeed,' she replied in matter-of-fact tones. 'Shall we go elsewhere to discuss it?'

He recollected himself then and spoke once more, this time lowering his voice. 'I cannot stand by and do nothing while Alice is forced into marriage with that . . . that tub of lard! I am going to approach her mother and ask for her hand.'

Fliss quite forgot that James had not previously been privy to discussions concerning Richard's affairs and she said in urgent tones, 'Richard, pray reflect a little. You cannot know . . .'

'What I know is that I love Alice and she loves me,' interrupted Richard. He, too, had clearly forgotten the need for discretion. 'If I do nothing, I shall run mad. I shall go back to Nick's lodging and smarten myself up. Then I shall attend Lady Susan and ask for permission to address Alice.'

'Richard, please!' begged Fliss. 'There must be something else . . .'

'Must there? Well, if there is, perhaps you will tell me what it may be, for I am sure I cannot think of it! There is no other honourable course for me and you know it.' He turned to go. Fliss went to put a hand on his arm, but to her surprise, Sir James put out his hand and quietly restrained her.

'Let him go,' he said. 'I know you want to save him from hurt, but you can't. He's not a little boy; he's a man! And he is right: it is the only honourable course.'

'Yes I know, but . . .' began Fliss, and then, to her horror, she felt tears springing to her eyes.

'Come,' said Sir James quickly. 'Suddenly I feel an almost over-mastering desire to visit the Abbey!' It was only a stone's throw from the Pump Room to the Abbey and in the ancient place of worship, often very busy but just now mercifully quiet, she regained her equilibrium.

'Thank you, James,' she said eventually. 'You are too good to me.'

'It is my pleasure to serve you and all your family,' he replied evenly. His carefully neutral tone further calmed her spirits, even whilst something about his words made her a little uncomfortable, although she could not have said exactly what it was at the time.

'You are right about Richard, of course,' she said after a tiny pause. 'He must decide these things for himself, and I know that I cannot protect him from the hurt that is bound to be his lot. But, oh, I do so wish that I could wave a magic wand and provide him with enough funds for him to become an eligible suitor.'

'Yes, that I do know,' replied Sir James harshly. 'Do you think I am blind and witless? You would sell everything you possess, including your diamond pendant over again, if it would save your brother from disappointment or disgrace.' Fliss gasped. She had not dreamed that James had guessed the reason why she had sold the only valuable piece of jewellery that she owned. James, seeing her surprise, went on in the same manner, 'Don't look so surprised! It was easy for me to guess that you needed the money for Richard.'

'But how?' she asked him. 'I was so careful, thought I was so discreet.'

'Why else would you suddenly need funds when he had only just appeared on the scene?' he asked. He was silent for a moment, then went on with an impatient gesture, 'You know

151

my story. Do you imagine I cannot tell when a man has been gambling? It was written all over his face. If I had thought for one moment that he would ever gamble ruinously again, I wouldn't have provided a single penny, even to save him for your sake!'

Shocked beyond measure at his words, Fliss lifted her trembling hands to unfasten the clasp of her pendant, which she happened to be wearing that day.

'Take it back then,' she said, in a voice that trembled as much as her hands. 'I do not want to have what is not freely given. I never knew why you bought it in the first place!' Before she could unfasten it, he took hold of her hands and brought them down, squeezing them tightly before releasing them.

'Did you not?' he said. His tone was gentle once again, his face calm. 'Perhaps now is not the right time or place to tell you. Instead, I will ask you a question: you always want to protect everyone in your family. Tell me this— who protects you?' She looked up at him, and suddenly it seemed as if she was on the verge of discovering something vitally important. Before either of them could say more on this head, however, they overheard Mrs Grantham's voice saying to someone, 'My dear sir, never say you have not visited the Abbey!' Suddenly Fliss knew that she could not face her near neighbour at this point, however genial she might be.

'I think I shall walk home now,' she said hurriedly. 'I feel the need of some fresh air. Pray tell Mrs Salisbury that I have gone.'

Sir James made no effort to detain her, but simply said, 'There is more to say, but now is not the time. However, please promise me this: if you hear of Richard planning anything that you consider to be rash or foolhardy, you will tell me. It might be that my intervention will do some good.' Fliss nodded in agreement and hurried away, avoiding Mrs Grantham and her companion by only seconds. She felt in need of reflection, and certainly did not want to make polite conversation.

As she walked along the High Street and past the Guild Hall, she thought hard, not just about what James had said, but about the tone of his voice. Never had he spoken to her so harshly! She had not dreamed that he had guessed why she needed the money or about Richard's gambling. There had been moments in their conversation when he had seemed to hold her in contempt, but at other times his view of her had seemed to be quite otherwise. He had said that he had bought the pendant for her sake, it was true, but earlier in the conversation he had said that it was his pleasure to serve all her family. At the end of their conversation, he had refused to take back her pendant, and his manner had changed to one that was as gentle as his previous one had been harsh. Finally, he had said that there was more he wanted to say to her. Did he perhaps intend to berate her further on her protective manner towards Richard?

So deep in thought was she that she missed her turning down Bridge Street, and found herself well along Northgate Street. Recalling that she needed to purchase something in Milsom Street anyway, she decided to walk there and give herself a little more exercise. Besides, there were other things to think about apart from Sir James's manner towards her and one of them was Richard's predicament. Going over in her mind's eye the scene that had taken place in the Pump Room that morning, she could not imagine that there was the smallest chance of Richard's being given permission to court Alice whilst her mother thought there was a possibility of snaring Mr Paranforth. The sad thing was that Richard himself did not appear to see this—or perhaps he did, but closed his mind to it. Yes, James was undoubtedly right: Richard was a man and must be allowed to make his own decisions, but how she wished that she could protect him from the hurt that would certainly result from this one!

Her purchase made, she walked the rest of the way up Milsom Street, intending to turn right into George Street. It was here, in Edgar Buildings, that Lord Nick had taken the lodgings which he was sharing with Richard and Octavius Bonsor. As she reached the corner, she looked across the road at the buildings and stopped suddenly in her tracks. Coming out of one of the front doors was Melissa and she was escorted by Octavius. There was no sign of Ruth Stringer.

Fliss took a deep breath. Confronting Melissa in the street would do no good and might even provoke the very scandal that she was now at pains to avert. Seeing that they were intending to cross the road, she stepped quickly into the nearest shop and waited until they had gone by, then resumed her journey. She did not want to bump into them; she would rather save what she had to say until she and Melissa were alone.

Hurrying along George Street and then into Broad Street, her mind was now full, not of Sir James and Richard, but of Melissa. She cursed herself for being so preoccupied with her brother's problems that she had failed to think carefully enough about those of her sister. She had guessed that Melissa was interested in Octavius Bonsor, but had fooled herself into thinking that it was only a passing fancy. Never had she supposed that that interest would have led her into doing something so improper as entering a man's lodgings! She wondered how many times Melissa had visited Octavius there, and if she had ever been seen. On reflection, she decided that it was unlikely. Fliss had already discovered that scandal travelled like wildfire in Bath. and such a juicy titbit would almost certainly have got around. So involved was she with these thoughts that Mrs Grantham had to address her twice.

'Miss Wintershill, you are wool-gathering, I do declare!' she said merrily. 'Have you been shopping? I am about to show Mr Paranforth the wonders of Milsom Street!' Fliss looked at the gentleman upon whose arm Mrs Grantham was leaning, and recognized him as being the same man whom she had seen speaking to Lady Susan in the Pump Room. He bowed courteously as Mrs Grantham introduced them, and she had to acknowledge that he was by no means so ill-looking in the fresh air. His face had more colour and animation now, and although he was not a handsome man, he looked kindly and dependable and his smile was warm. He was undoubtedly Alice's senior by twenty-five years at least, but had Richard not been involved, Fliss could well see that given Alice's straitened circumstances, she could do a good deal worse for herself.

'Do you find Milsom Street a wonderful place, Miss Wintershill?' he asked with a twinkle. 'I am by no means convinced that a gentleman's view would be the same as a lady's in that respect!'

'You may have a point there, sir,' answered Fliss, trying to smile.

'Fie on you, Miss Wintershill!' exclaimed Mrs Grantham. 'When we all know that a lady is always right!'

Mr Paranforth sighed. 'Very well then, Amanda,' he said. 'Lead on. I will promise to admire everything you recommend.'

'No no, that will never do! I should be bored to death. I need an escort who will share in my interests, but still know his own mind. What do you say, Miss Wintershill?' Fliss was not at all in the mood for this kind of badinage, but she exerted herself to be agreeable.

'Why certainly, Mrs Grantham,' she answered. 'The only solution is that Mr Paranforth should state his opinion, but he must not by any means contradict you. In other words, he must agree with you all the time, but really mean it!'

Mr Paranforth passed a hand over his eyes. 'I think I had better lie down,' he murmured in failing accents.

'That might be as well, if you are to attend the ball at the Upper Rooms this evening,' replied Mrs Grantham. 'I believe your party is to go, Miss Wintershill?'

'We certainly plan to be there,' said Fliss. 'I hope I do not disgrace myself by forgetting the steps! I do not dance very much these days.'

'Oh, for shame, Miss Wintershill!' retorted Mrs Grantham. 'There is nothing for you to fear. The days of separate couples having to execute the minuet alone are, thank heaven, a thing of the past!'

'I am sure you will enjoy it very much,' said Mr Paranforth. 'I fear I must take my doctor's advice and cry off, however. Too many late nights are not to be attempted yet, I believe, particularly when he has told me that I must take the bath every morning. I wonder whether James might come to my hotel and play a hand of whist with me?' Fliss was surprised at the lurch of disappointment that she felt at these words.

'Certainly not,' declared Mrs Grantham. 'I am sure you can risk an hour or two, Edgar. And in any case, you cannot possibly deprive us of such a fine dancer as James. Miss Wintershill, lend me your support!' Fliss blushed, to her great annoyance, murmured something non-committal, then hurriedly made her excuses and left them. She now had to admit to herself that she was strongly attracted to James, and could think of no one with whom she would rather dance. Bad enough that this should be so, without Mrs Grantham guessing it, and teasing her on the subject.

CHAPTER TWELVE

On her arrival back in Laura Place, Fliss went immediately upstairs, knocked on Melissa's door and with very little ceremony, walked in. Melissa was sitting at a table in the window reading a note, and when she looked up and saw her sister, she hurriedly folded it and put it away. The very secretive nature of this action on the part of one with whom until recently she had been sharing a bedroom, caused Fliss's anger, already bubbling under the surface, to spill over.

'Not content then, with meeting Octavius Bonsor at his lodging, you must needs receive notes from him too! Melissa, I thought better of you.' At this, Melissa turned pale, but she met her sister's gaze steadily.

'What makes you think that I have been meeting Octavius?' she said, getting up.

'Oh Lissa, I saw you come out of his lodging in his company.'

'You are forgetting that it is also Richard's lodging,' retorted Melissa, remaining where she was. 'Did it not occur to you that I might be visiting our brother?'

'No, it didn't,' said Fliss frankly. 'And it still doesn't sound very likely to me.'

'Well, it is true,' flashed Melissa. 'I'm not lying, and you needn't accuse me of it!'

Fliss sighed in exasperation. 'But why on earth should you need to go there?' she asked. 'You had seen him in the Pump Room less than an hour before. A message would find him if your business was so urgent. You know perfectly well that you should not be visiting a man in his lodgings, whoever he may be.'

'I don't see why I should explain myself to you when you obviously think the worst of me, but I will do so, otherwise you might go telling tales to Mama. I met Richard by chance outside his lodgings. He was so agitated that I insisted he tell me what was the matter, only he would not do so in the open street, so I went in with him. He told me all about Alice Tryon, and about how he is trying to pluck up his courage to offer for her. I tried to calm him down, then Octavius came in and was as prim as you are about my being there at all. He insisted on escorting me home. It was just bad luck that you saw us.'

'Yes, and it would have been very bad luck if anyone else had seen you,' retorted Fliss. 'We have no fortunes. If we lose our reputations, what do we have left?' She was silent for a moment, then went on, 'Lissa, I want you to be honest with me: have you been meeting Octavius Bonsor in his lodgings?'

'I don't know why I should bother to answer,' replied her sister, turning her head away. 'You have clearly convinced yourself that I have.'

Fliss sighed. 'That isn't so. It's just that, well, I could not help but notice that you have been drawn towards him. I thought that your inclination for him might have led you into indiscretion.' When Melissa was still silent, Fliss said, 'Please, Lissa?'

'Very well,' Melissa said, wearily. 'If it makes you happy, I will swear to you that I have not been meeting Octavius in his

160

lodgings.' Fliss went over to her then and took her hands.

'This is not to make me happy; it's so that I can discover how to help you.' She paused. 'I am on your side, you know.'

Melissa smiled faintly. 'Yes, I know. Truly, Fliss, I have not been meeting Octavius. And the note was not from him either. Do you want to read it?'

Fliss shook her head. 'I am not Mama, and I have no wish to intrude upon your privacy, and no right to do so either. If you say it is not from Octavius, then that is enough for me. Shall I come back later to help you dress for the ball?'

*   *   *

Richard arrived at the house that evening to escort them to the assembly rooms, looking very handsome in a dark-blue coat with snowy white breeches, and white waistcoat embroidered with silver thread. While Melissa and Mrs Salisbury were exchanging a few words, Richard managed to say to her, 'I've been thinking things over, and perhaps I have been a little hasty. After all, Paranforth clearly isn't well; one only has to look at his complexion to see that! Anyway, I don't want to spoil things by rushing, so I mean to wait for a little while and see.'

'Oh Richard, I'm so glad,' answered Fliss

giving his arm a little squeeze. 'I heard him telling Mrs Grantham only today that he was to take the bath as well as drink the waters, so maybe that's why he's here after all.'

'I don't intend to wait for ever, though,' he warned her. 'I am thinking of speaking to her mother in a week's time. Mind you, if I think that he's coming close to a declaration, I'll pop my proposal in quick. After all, we're a good family, and I shall be the squire when Father . . . I mean, that is, I shall be the squire one day.' Fliss smiled at him. She could not be optimistic about his chances, but she did not want to do or say anything to shake this more hopeful mood. 'Anyway,' he went on, 'both you and Melissa warned me against rushing into things so I suppose I ought to take some notice.'

'You shouldn't have encouraged Melissa to go into your lodgings, though, Richard,' said Fliss, suddenly reminded of the afternoon's incident. 'And you certainly shouldn't have allowed her to leave with Octavius.'

'No, I'm sorry, I didn't think, I was so agitated about Alice,' confessed Richard. 'I shan't do it again.' Fliss said no more on the subject. If, as she hoped, no one but herself had been witness to the incident, then there was no harm done. If someone *had* seen, then they would discover soon enough—probably at the ball.

Luck appeared to have favoured them on

this occasion, however. There was plenty of scandal circulating, but none of it concerned Melissa. Fliss did hear a rumour that Lord Nick had found himself a new flirt, but he seemed to have no inclination to dally with anyone in particular that evening. Mr Paranforth did appear, but he did not dance, and spent only an hour in the card room before returning to his hotel. This meant that Richard was able to enjoy the evening with unmixed feelings. He danced two dances with Alice, but made no attempt to ask for more, and Fliss was pleased to see that he also danced with Ruth Stringer, among others, and resisted the temptation of sitting in Alice's pocket for the evening.

Nick and Octavius wandered in together, and for a moment stood side by side in the doorway, Nick dressed in a coat in his favourite hue of deep purple, and Octavius, like Richard, in blue. Even their stance was similar and they looked amazingly alike. Fliss happened to be standing next to her sister, and she turned to her, commenting on the likeness.

'Yes, they are alike, aren't they?' agreed Melissa. 'I could hardly believe it when I first saw Lord Octavius—side by side with his brother, I mean.'

The two brothers were followed in almost immediately by Sir James, escorting Mrs Grantham.

'Here we are, Miss Wintershill,' declared

Mrs Grantham. 'I have been telling James about how anxious you are concerning the dancing, and he has promised to look after you. You could not have a more capable partner, I assure you. And now, I must seek out Edgar, as I told him that I would give him a hand of cards this evening.' She drifted away, leaving Fliss and James standing looking at one another.

'I would be delighted if you would honour me with a dance,' said James. Fliss had already decided that she would very much like to dance with him, but she did not want him to offer on Mrs Grantham's instructions, so she said,

'Pray do not feel obliged to do so, sir; I am not so desperate a case as that.' His face changed from one of courteous attentiveness to one of offended rigidity.

'Forgive me, ma'am,' he said coldly. 'No doubt there are other men with whom you would much rather dance. I would not dream of cluttering up your dance card!' With that, he bowed stiffly and walked away. Fliss looked after him, appalled. She had never intended her words to be meant in such a way. Moments later, before she could decide whether to go after him, or hope for a chance of explaining later, Lord Nick approached her, and asked her to dance. Fliss looked round and noticed that Octavius was leading Melissa on to the floor, and that James had clearly persuaded

Mrs Grantham to delay her card game, for they were preparing to dance together. Smiling in a rather strained way, she put her hand into that of the rakish nobleman and allowed him to lead her on to the floor for a set of country dances.

'I could have sworn that you were going to dance with James,' murmured Nick provocatively.

'No . . . yes . . . that is, I . . . He asked, but I . . . I expect that . . .'

Lord Nick listened with courteous interest. 'Not one of your more lucid comments,' he remarked, when there was clearly no more to come. Fliss had to laugh then, despite herself.

'There was a foolish misunderstanding,' she said at last. 'I expressed myself badly, and James decided that I meant I did not want to dance with him.'

'I'll have a word with him after the set,' promised Nick. 'It would not do for you to be pining away.'

'I will not pine away!' exclaimed Fliss. 'Good heavens, what a fuss just because a man does not really . . . that is, does not want to dance with me! I pray that you will say nothing at all!'

'Ah!' said Nick in the tones of one who has made a great discovery.

'Nick, I forbid you to say anything!' cried Fliss. 'Please—just leave it be.'

'How can I possibly refuse a lady who has

just done something that I have been wanting her to do ever since I met her?' he said impishly.

'My Lord?' she asked.

'You have called me by my Christian name. Now I really shall have something to tell James!' When the dance was over, Nick led Fliss back to her chair, bowed gracefully, and made his way over to James's side. Almost immediately, Fliss was addressed by a Mrs Adamson who was acquainted with her mother, so she was unable to do other than cast an anguished glance in Nick's direction and pray that he did not say anything too outrageous. Whatever it was, it could not have been to James's liking, for he kept his distance for the rest of the evening.

The following week was not one of unalloyed enjoyment for Fliss. On the one hand, she loved being in Bath, attending concerts and parties and shopping and just being free of household concerns. On the other, wherever James was, there Mrs Grantham seemed to be, and she had to admit to finding this disturbing. There had been no obvious opportunity to explain her comment in the assembly rooms, and now she felt that she could hardly refer to that occasion without it sounding decidedly odd. Her one consolation was that Mrs Grantham and Sir James often appeared to be accompanied by Mr Paranforth. This circumstance pleased

166

Richard too. He became convinced that Mr Paranforth had simply come to Bath to take the waters and had never had a thought of marriage on his mind.

'After all,' he said to Fliss, as the end of the week drew near, 'it stands to reason that he cannot be so enamoured of Alice if he is keeping his distance. I shall definitely offer for Alice now.' Fliss said nothing, but felt doubtful. A man of Paranforth's years and experience would know better than to make a nuisance of himself around a girl all the time. And after all, although people might talk of love matches, it was a fact of life that in the case of an under-aged girl without fortune, her opinion mattered less than that of her mother.

The day that Richard had chosen to make his offer was the same day on which there was to be a firework display at the Sydney Gardens in the evening. He got up bright and early, then realized that he could hardly pay a visit of form at nine o'clock in the morning. Octavius and Nick were still in bed, so he went out to stroll around a little. There was a jeweller's shop in Milsom Street, and he stopped outside, wondering whether to go in and take a look at rings. He certainly needed to speak to Mama first before making a purchase, as there might be a family ring which ought to go to the bride of the eldest son, but it would do no harm to look all the same.

Once inside he found that he was obliged to

wait because a lady and gentleman were already being served. He soon realized that they were Mr Paranforth and Mrs Grantham, and they, also, were looking at rings.

'But it is your money, Edgar,' Mrs Grantham was saying. 'Yours must be the final choice.'

'Not at all,' replied Paranforth. 'Come; I insist that you choose.' He smiled at the assistant. 'Nothing is too good for my bride to be.'

'Bride to be!' said Mrs Grantham, archly. 'When I have it on good authority that you have not yet made a formal proposal!'

'Have patience, my dear,' answered Paranforth in a similar tone. 'Be assured that when I do make a formal proposal, you will be the very first to know.'

Richard did not wait to hear any more, but hurried out of the shop. So it was true after all! Paranforth was to offer for Alice and was even buying a ring. But if the formal proposal had not been made, he still had a chance. He must make his own offer without delay.

*   *   *

They had been singularly well-blessed for weather during their stay in Bath, and that evening proved to be no exception. The firework display in the Sydney Gardens was to be the first of the season, and was somewhat

168

early in the year, but clearly it had been decided that there were enough notables in Bath to make the effort worthwhile.

As they made ready to walk the short distance from Laura Place, Fliss could not but reflect how easily simple conversations could poison the prospect of even such a novel entertainment as that which presently awaited her.

She had had a rather disturbing encounter with Melissa, when she had popped in to help her to get ready. Melissa had obviously taken great care with her appearance, and seemed very excited. This did not surprise Fliss; she was feeling quite excited herself. She could not help feeling suspicious, however, that her sister's excitement might have something to do with the possible presence of Octavius Bonsor. Melissa had assured her the previous week that she had not been meeting the young lieutenant, and Fliss would not stoop to doubt her. But she found herself feeling rather uneasy when she had looked in the mirror and caught sight of Melissa looking at her with an expression that was almost calculating. Then, almost at the very moment when she had noticed it, it was gone and she simply said, 'Who is to be of our party this evening, Fliss?'

'Oh, just ourselves, Mrs Salisbury, Sir James and . . . and Mrs Grantham, I think.'

'Oh, yes. She certainly seems to know him very well, doesn't she? Do you think that they might make a match of it, Fliss?' Fliss had made some non-committal remark, and changed the subject very quickly. Melissa clearly did not need any help, so Fliss whisked herself out of the room with some excuse about having forgotten to put a handkerchief in her reticule. Once back in her room, she found that she did not want to be alone with her thoughts, so calling through to Melissa that she would wait for her downstairs, she went down to the drawing-room to find her hostess giving instructions to a footman who was to follow with extra shawls, in case the evening should prove to be chilly.

'How charming you look, my dear,' said Mrs Salisbury after the man had gone. She was looking very attractive herself in a cloak of dark blue with a bonnet with matching ribbons. 'We only await your sister, and James and Mrs Grantham who are to walk with us.' She looked around and dropped her voice, for all the world as if she expected there to be spies behind the curtains or under the table. 'Mrs Grantham confided in me this afternoon that she has hopes of being married soon. What a fine thing that will be for James! He has been alone for too long. And of course, there is no question of his needing an heir, because he already has William, so he may marry whom he pleases. How nice it will be for you, my dear, to have such a congenial neighbour! I dare say you will be visiting one another all the time!' Melissa came in at this point and Mrs Salisbury exclaimed, 'Oh my dear, what a pretty cloak! But there is a tiny mark on the shoulder which I think may be dust. Do let me see if I can brush it off for you.'

Fliss left them and wandered over to the window to look out over the dark street. She was glad of the diversion for it meant that her hostess would not wonder why she was suddenly looking so pale. Mrs Grantham popping up everywhere had made her feel uncomfortable, but she had not been able to understand why. Now she suddenly realized that if Mrs Grantham married Sir James, then life in their little neighbourhood would no longer be tolerable. How could she possibly bear seeing them together, now that she had discovered that she was in love with him?

Moments later, the doorbell rang and Yare admitted the very two people about whom she had just been thinking. At sight of James, she could feel herself turning bright red and she could barely greet them with equanimity.

'My dear Miss Wintershill!' exclaimed Mrs Grantham. 'You look quite flushed! Are you sure you are well?'

'Yes, thank you,' replied Fliss, thankful that even if she had no control over her complexion, she could at least control her voice. 'I suppose I must have hurried down the stairs.' She caught a glimpse of James looking at her steadily, but he said nothing beyond the usual polite greeting.

Soon it was time for them all to leave the house. To Fliss's surprise, Mrs Grantham chose to walk with Mrs Salisbury, and James offered one arm to Fliss and the other to Melissa. It was not the first time that she had taken his arm, but this time, with her feelings for him awakened, she seemed conscious of his presence and the feel of him as never before. What would she do now if he married Mrs Grantham? Her first instinct was to run away, but she knew that that was impossible. Where could she go? In any case, how would the family manage without her? She would simply have to school herself to think of James as just a friend. The trouble was, that that was all he had been to her for a long time. Having now begun to think of him in another way, she did not see how she could ever go back to how things were.

She heaved a sigh and James, looking down at her and thinking that she was worrying about Richard, said in a low tone, 'Try not to be anxious. You have done all you can for him.' Fliss did not correct him, but merely smiled. She looked around and, to her surprise, she realized that she had been so absorbed in her thoughts that they had reached the Sydney Gardens already. It was far busier than Fliss had ever seen it. Many other people had obviously been similarly

172

drawn by the mild weather to take in the spectacle.

'Only fancy,' exclaimed Mrs Salisbury, 'had we come here thirty years ago, we would have had to be ferried across the river in order to get here. Now would not that have been romantic?'

'My dear Elvira,' replied James, 'I cannot think that any boat trip in your company would be in the slightest degree romantic. When we went on a boat on Windermere when we were twelve, you were violently sick, and when you visited me at university and I took you on the Cam, you threw my hat in the water.'

'James, you are far too selective in your memories,' replied Mrs Salisbury. 'I protest, it would have been charming.'

Just then, Melissa noticed Ruth Stringer and her party and asked permission to join them. Fliss, feeling that she had been rather unfair to her sister that day, readily agreed, but added, 'I will come and have a word with Mrs Makepiece.'

'To make sure that I don't arrange an assignation with Octavius Bonsor?' asked Melissa defiantly.

'Of course not,' replied Fliss. 'But Mrs Makepiece has been very kind, and it seems only right to thank her for all the hospitality that she has extended to you.'

'Oh all right,' said Melissa ungraciously, but she did look a little shame-faced. Mrs

Makepiece exchanged courtesies with Fliss in a friendly manner and assured her that Melissa was no trouble to her.

'I often think that it is easier to look after two than one,' she said. 'Then they can keep one another amused.' They exchanged a few more commonplaces, whilst Ruth and Melissa chattered together. 'I will see her safely home after the display if we do not find you,' promised Ruth's aunt. Fliss thanked her, and turned back to rejoin her party. She had not gone more than three or four steps, when she felt a tap on her shoulder and she turned to see Richard standing close to her. His face looked ghastly in the pale-blue light close to him, and his chin jutted defiantly.

'I'm glad I've found you, Fliss,' he said in the tones of someone who is determined to keep in control, however strong his emotions. 'You were right, of course. I went to see Lady Susan, but she barely listened to me. I don't think she even took my offer seriously. She looked as if she begrudged the time that it took to put down her needlework. She has set her mind on Paranforth, that's certain.'

'Has he offered for her?' asked Fliss.

'From what Lady Susan said, the matter is as good as settled,' he replied. 'Alice's birthday is next week. The engagement is to be announced then. Alice is to be sacrificed on the altar of her mother's greed.'

'Oh Richard, I'm so sorry,' cried Fliss, her

174

heart going out to him even more, now that she knew what it was like to feel love that was surely doomed to disappointment.

'Don't be,' he said firmly, drawing himself up. 'I'm not going to let it happen.'

'What do you mean?' asked Fliss apprehensively. 'You aren't going to do anything rash—'

'There's only one way of stopping it now,' he replied resolutely. 'Alice and I are eloping.'

'Richard!' she gasped. 'You can't!'

'Why not?' he asked recklessly. 'I've tried the honourable approach and it didn't work. What else can I do? Stand by and watch whilst Alice is married to another man? Think of her having to share his home, his bed? No. I won't do it.'

'Richard, there must be another way,' she pleaded.

'Then tell me what it is. Now.' She was silent. 'You see? There isn't another way. We're leaving tonight, from here. I have a carriage arranged. We'll never get a better chance. I've only told you because of all you've done for me.' He gave her a quick hug. 'Wish me happy!'

'Oh, I do, but . . .' It was too late. He was gone. For a moment, that was all that she could take in. Then into her mind came rushing many jumbled thoughts concerning the disgrace of an elopement, pursuit and possible duels, Alice's ruined reputation, the effect of scandal upon Richard's career prospects, and the grave shock that it would be to her mother and father. What could she do? Suddenly, she recalled James's voice saying 'If you hear of Richard planning anything rash, tell me'. She looked around, half expecting to see him, so clear had his voice been in her head, but there was no sign of him. Anxious to find him, she ran in the direction nearest to where she had last seen him. This led her briefly down an unfrequented path and she stopped for a moment to look around and get her bearings. As she did so, she saw a couple locked in a passionate embrace and, as they drew apart briefly, light fell on the young woman's face. It was Melissa. The man, whose face was in shadow, looked to be Octavius Bonsor.

Fliss took a deep breath, then ran on. She could not possibly think about her sister's deceitfulness now. That would have to be dealt with later. Just now, the most urgent need was to save Richard and Alice from disgrace. As she reached the end of the path, she cannoned into a man standing there, nearly knocking him over. As he turned, she saw to her relief that it was James.

'Good grief, it's another invasion,' he declared in an amused voice. Then as he caught sight of her face, his tone changed and he said urgently, 'Felicity what is it? What has happened?'

'It's Richard,' she said, almost sobbing with

relief at having found him so quickly. 'He's eloping with Alice—tonight!'

'I take it that Lady Susan refused him, as predicted?'

Fliss nodded. 'He has decided to take what he thinks is the only way out,' she replied.

'Did he say if they were leaving from here?' he asked her.

'Yes, they are. He just came to say goodbye to me.' She could feel a sob rising in her throat as she finished speaking. 'Oh, James, can you do anything?'

'Don't worry. Leave it to me. I'll stop them,' he said reassuringly. 'You go and join the others—they're over there,' he said, gesturing towards a knot of people. He was about to leave her when Lord Nick appeared from behind where Fliss was standing.

'I believe I can guess what's toward, Miss Wintershill,' he said. 'Your brother and my niece have decided to declare the world well lost for love—never a sensible course, in my opinion. I'll go with you, James. Alice will need somebody.' The two of them hurried off toward the entrance. She stood watching them helplessly for a moment or two, then because she could not think what else to do, she did as he bade her and walked over to join Mrs Salisbury and Mrs Grantham.

'Oh there you are,' exclaimed Mrs Salisbury. 'I was afraid that we might have lost you, such a press of persons as there is here tonight.'

'Is this your first visit to the Sydney Gardens, Miss Wintershill?' asked Mrs Grantham. Fliss found herself replying courteously that she had visited them by day, but never before by night, but inside, she was almost screaming with the absurdity of having to conduct this polite social conversation whilst there were events taking place so close to them that might determine more than two people's happiness. Lovely music played and fireworks went off, but Fliss was oblivious to it all. The only thing that did recall her to the present was when suddenly she happened to see Melissa by her side. At once she remembered seeing her with Octavius, but now was not the moment to challenge her, especially since Ruth Stringer and her aunt were nearby. Until Richard's affairs were settled, she could think of nothing else.

All at once, she was conscious of a presence behind her and turning round, she saw James. He was alone. She opened her mouth to speak, but before she could say anything, he murmured, 'All's well. We found them in time. Nick is taking care of Alice.' She closed her eyes in relief. He took hold of her hand and gave it a little squeeze, then released it. She wished that she could have held on to him for ever.

At last she said, 'I want to speak to Richard.'

'I'm not at all sure that that would be wise,'

he replied carefully.

'Why not? He will be distressed about the failure of the elopement. I am always the one to whom he turns.' All at once she caught sight of Richard and immediately started pushing through the crowd in order to reach him.

She heard James say behind her, 'Felicity, wait!' But she hurried on regardless, thinking only that she must reach Richard's side. At last, quite breathless, she got to him. He was standing on his own, a little apart from the crowd.

'Richard,' she said. He turned to look at her and his face was as she had never seen it before, contorted into a savage mask of fury.

'It was you! I knew that it must have been you who betrayed us the minute that Singleton turned up.'

'Yes Richard, I had to! I—'

'Had to? Why? Couldn't you bear anyone else to have some happiness? Rupert died, so you've been left on the shelf! Have you turned into such a bitter old spinster that you can't stand the idea of my marrying the girl of my choice?'

'No, Richard! It was for your sake—yours and Alice's.'

'For our sakes? Don't make me laugh. It was to satisfy your own desire always to be in charge of our family, always to do everything. And don't think I don't realize why it was Singleton that you made use of. You're hoping to catch him for yourself, aren't you? Well you haven't a chance. Grantham's snared him right enough, and if she hasn't yet, she soon will. And I hope that when you see them together you hurt as much inside as I'm hurting now.'

Fliss stared at him, too stunned and horrified to speak. He stood looking at her for a moment, his expression filled with hatred and pain. Then, without another word, he turned on his heel and left her. She stood watching him go. Her limbs seemed to have been turned to stone. She wanted to run after him, but somehow she could not work out how to put one foot in front of another. Then, mercifully, she felt behind her the same presence as before, and James was there, his hands on her shoulders.

At once, everything was too much for her and the tears began to run down her face. Quickly but firmly, James drew her away from the crowds and into the shelter of the trees, away from prying eyes. There, in the kindest and gentlest way possible, he pulled her into a comforting embrace, and allowed her to cry on his shoulder. At first, all that she could think of was the way in which Richard had spoken to her with cruel words, calculated to wound her. Then, as she grew calmer, she suddenly became conscious that she was in James's arms.

Feeling her sobs subside, he held her at arm's length and said, 'Feeling better?'

She managed to muster a smile, even though his moving away gave her an acute feeling of loss, and she said in an unsteady voice, 'A little.'

'Good girl,' he said and, drawing her close again, he kissed her forehead then, after a little hesitation, her cheek. Suddenly, for Fliss it was not enough. The pain of Richard's words, his looks, his rejection, still hovered at the back of her mind, and she needed very badly to drive the pain away. As James's breath was still warm on her cheek from his chaste salute, she turned her head so that their lips met, touched and clung briefly. Her eyes were closed, but she heard James take a ragged breath then felt his kisses brief, even gentle, but increasingly urgent as he saluted both her cheeks, the hollow beneath her ear, and her mouth once more, this time more firmly. He would have released her then. She could feel him drawing away, but that she could not bear. All thoughts of propriety disappeared as she slid her arms around his neck and pulled his head down towards hers. This time, with a groan, he covered her mouth with his and kissed her long and hard, and she kissed him back until it would have been impossible to say who was kissing whom.

At length they drew apart, but just as James was saying, 'Felicity, I . . .' they heard the voice of Mrs Salisbury saying to Mrs Grantham, 'He came this way I am sure. He must be here somewhere.'

Suddenly, Fliss remembered that James was as good as promised to Mrs Grantham, and that she was just an unwanted spinster throwing herself at someone else's man. With a cry, she tore herself free and for the second time that evening ran away from James, this time towards the entrance. She paid no heed to the curious glances that followed her. Her only concern was to reach the sanctuary of her room and then, if possible, to make arrangements so that she would never have to clap eyes on James, or Mrs Grantham, or even Richard, for the rest of her life.

On her arrival at Laura Place, Yare admitted her, not looking as surprised as might have been expected. When Fliss looked beyond him, she realized that he had had other things to think about, for standing in the hall was her brother Christopher.

'Chris, oh Chris!' she exclaimed running to him. He caught her in a warm embrace, but he did not seem to have any of his usual exuberance. 'What brings you to Bath?' she asked eventually. But when she looked at his serious face, she knew what he was going to say before he opened his mouth. 'Mama?' she faltered. He nodded.

'I've come to fetch you home,' he said. 'The baby came too early—a little girl. Mama and the baby both died this morning.'

CHAPTER THIRTEEN

Fliss sighed. At last, everyone in the family had now been provided with mourning black. She and Melissa were able to share the gowns that Mama herself had worn when Ross and Paul had died ten years before. The others were all dressed in a similar way from mourning clothes that had been put in store.

It was odd, she reflected to herself, how the house did not appear to be any different. When Christopher had brought them back the day after the firework party, she had somehow expected that the family's loss would be in some way discernible in the brickwork, but everything looked just the same. Even her role had not changed. Mistress of the house for so long in everything but name, she slipped into that position without difficulty. She also returned to being the squire's steward, since Christopher went back to university immediately after the funeral. Her father seemed perceptibly older. He did not indulge in any excesses, but appeared lost and lacking in any vitality and he leaned on her more than ever.

To the little ones, who had barely known their mother as an active person, there was no change. The older ones cried on Fliss's shoulder and expected her to make everything better, and she did her best, but there seemed to be no one with whom she could share her own grief, no one's shoulder upon which *she* could cry. However hard she tried to be sensible, she could not help looking back longingly to the time she had spent in Bath. It had been marvellous to be able to enjoy a life without heavy responsibility: more than anything, it had been lovely to feel that if only for a short time, in James, she had had someone upon whom she could lean. It seemed now like a story that she had read of someone else's life.

She had hardly seen James to speak to since the night of their visit to the Sydney Gardens. He had brought Mrs Salisbury, Mrs Grantham and Melissa home and had listened gravely to Christopher's tidings.

'I am so very sorry,' he had said. 'More sorry than I can express. You will be wishing to leave Bath as soon as possible.'

'First thing in the morning, sir,' Christopher had replied, feeling very adult, what with the grave nature of his errand, and the fact that Melissa had chosen to weep on his shoulder. 'Just as soon as I can hire a carriage.'

'As to that, sir, my carriage is naturally at your disposal,' Sir James had said politely, thus increasing Christopher's confidence tenfold. He had then turned to Fliss. 'Is there anything else I may have the honour of doing for you?'

'If you could find Richard and inform him

of what has happened, I should be very grateful,' Fliss had answered. To her shame, she could only think, as she looked at him, of how he had held her in his arms earlier, and wish that it could be possible for him to do the same now.

'You may depend on me,' he had said, bowing. 'Pray convey to your father my deepest sympathies. I will, of course, be calling on him in person as soon as I have brought Richard to you.' Mrs Grantham had sent a similar message, then the two of them had left together. Fliss had watched his retreating back and wished that she had the right to lean upon him.

The following morning, rising betimes after a restless night, Fliss had gone to her sister's room and found it empty. Expecting to find her at breakfast, Fliss went downstairs herself but found only Mrs Salisbury at table.

'Perhaps she needed some fresh air,' said her hostess doubtfully.

'Well, I hope she doesn't want too much,' answered Fliss rather tartly. 'We must be off in an hour.' Mrs Salisbury laid her hand sympathetically on one of Fliss's.

'My dear, I am so sorry about your news,' she said seriously, 'and I am more sorry to lose you than I can say. But perhaps James may bring you to stay with me again. I can promise you that you will be very welcome.' Fliss smiled, but in her heart she was sure that she would never return. Now that she had had time to think, she was covered with shame at the way in which she had clung to James and invited his kisses. His intention had clearly been only to comfort her; it was she who had brazenly forced herself upon him. Once he had followed his own inclination and married Mrs Grantham, there would be no more chances for her to come back to stay with his aunt in Bath.

Whilst they were still at breakfast, they heard the sound of the front door knocker, the door being opened and closed, and then footsteps running upstairs.

'That must be Melissa,' said Fliss. 'I'll go upstairs and see if she wants any breakfast.'

There was a touch of urgency about the footsteps that made her a little uneasy. She went to Melissa's bedroom door and tapped softly. There was no answer so she tapped again, saying, 'Lissa it's me, Fliss. Are you all right?' Suddenly the door flew open, and Melissa stood on the threshold. There was a tension in her expression that Fliss did not like. 'Lissa, are you all right?' she asked again. 'Why did you need to go out? I heard you running up the stairs.'

'Can I do nothing without . . .' began Melissa, with an explosion of anger that Fliss could not remember hearing from her sister before. Then she broke off and said, 'Yes . . . yes, of course, I am all right. I just wanted to

186

tell Ruth Stringer that we are leaving.'

'I see,' said Fliss. 'Did you manage to give your message?'

'My message?' said Melissa a little wildly. 'Oh . . . yes, yes, I saw her. She is very sorry. Fliss, I have not yet finished packing. May I . . . ?'

'Oh . . . oh yes, of course,' said Fliss quickly. She stepped back, and Melissa closed the door. Not so long ago, they had helped each other to pack in order to come here; today, Fliss definitely felt that Melissa preferred her absence to her presence. She wondered whether in fact her sister had hoped to see Octavius Bonsor, but had not managed to do so. Certainly, she had not acted like a girl who had just seen the man she loved, albeit before an absence that could well be prolonged.

Since arriving home, Melissa had gone about her duties efficiently enough, but she looked rather pale and gave the impression that a large part of her mind was elsewhere. Fliss had never challenged her sister about the embrace that she had witnessed in the Sydney Gardens. The moment was past, and no one else had seen what had taken place. Melissa was clearly suffering enough, without any intervention from her older sister.

Two days after their arrival from Bath, Richard had returned with Sir James. His manner towards Fliss was reserved, but the shock of their mother's death and the need to deal with everything involved with it took precedence over what had taken place between them. There had been no change in Melissa's mood since Richard's arrival, so obviously he had brought her no message from Octavius. Clearly he had deserted her, for Richard would surely have told him about their mother's death: and what faithful lover would have stayed away at such a time?

In accordance with accepted custom, only the men of the household attended the funeral. Sir James and other local gentlemen went in order to pay their respects and returned to the house afterwards for refreshments. As Fliss watched him talking quietly with her father, she almost wondered whether she had imagined the passionate kiss that they had shared, so widely removed did it seem from the present. The lurch that her heart gave when she saw the baronet told her that whatever else she might have imagined, there was no doubt that her love for him was real. Before he left, he came over to speak to her. The black coat he wore set off his broad shoulders superbly, and she scolded herself inwardly for noticing such a thing even while she was in mourning.

'I think you may find that Richard is a little more reconciled to your actions,' he said in a lowered tone. 'I have tried to explain to him something of your motives, but I cannot say more on that head without breaking confidence with him. However, I wanted to tell you what I had done because I have had letters from my Lincolnshire estate and there is business that demands my immediate attention.' The news that he was going away filled her with such dismay that for a moment, as she looked up at him, her feelings were written clearly on her face. He took a step closer and began to speak rapidly and with more urgency. 'My dear, there are things I want so much to say to you, but just now I . . .' At that moment, Dr Winkliffe, who had attended Mrs Wintershill in her last illness, came to join them and the moment was lost. Before he left the house, James found time to say, 'I only expect to be gone a week. If it is to be longer, I shall write to you.'

A week later, a letter came for Richard from Octavius Bonsor. It arrived whilst they were all at the breakfast-table and, although he looked a little pale as he took it, he did not open it.

'I'll read it later,' he said. Fliss noticed that Melissa's eyes were fixed on the letter with a kind of pitiful intensity, and her heart sank. Obviously her sister was still obsessed with the handsome young lieutenant.

Once breakfast was over, the family went their separate ways. Melissa looked very reluctant to take some of the children for a drawing lesson, but she went all the same. Fliss felt bound to wonder whether her pupils would

189

learn anything worthwhile with their older sister in her present mood, but she had too many tasks of her own to take that one off Melissa's shoulders. She was busy sorting out her accounts when Richard came bounding in.

As James had predicted, he had been less hostile than she would have supposed during the last few days. He had certainly been reserved and quiet, but then so had they all been with Mama's death occupying their minds. Now, he looked happier than she had seen him for a long time.

'What is it, Richard?' she asked him, laying down her pen with a smile. 'Have you had good news?'

'Very good news,' he replied happily. 'I have heard from Octavius, and apparently Paranforth did not propose! Tavy thinks that he had some other female in his eye. I know myself that he was thinking seriously of someone, for I saw Mrs Grantham helping him to choose a ring. Tavy says that he was probably just being polite on account of having been a friend of Alice's father, who died four years ago.'

'You have a reprieve, in short,' said Fliss. 'Richard, I am so glad.'

'You mean that Alice has had a reprieve. They are fixed in Bath for the time being, since Lady Susan cannot afford another London season for Alice.' He paused for a moment. 'I feel rather mean, rejoicing in her

190

lack of success, but I just can't help it!'

'Richard, did you really only receive a letter from Octavius?' asked Fliss teasingly. Richard grinned.

'Alice is an angel,' he replied. 'I am determined to marry her, and I don't mean to waste any time either. Sir James has offered to introduce me to someone who may be able to get me a diplomatic posting and that should render me more eligible, for I can't hope for quick advancement or prize money in the navy while we are at peace. He's a splendid fellow, isn't he? He's asked me to call him James by the way. He says I'm by far too old now to be calling him by his title.'

'Yes, he is splendid,' replied Fliss, wondering whether James had asked her to call him by his Christian name simply because he thought she was old as well. 'Richard, I am sorry that I betrayed your confidence, but I could not think what else to do. I felt sure that when your head was cool, you would regret running the risk of involving Alice in scandal.'

Richard smiled ruefully. 'You were right, of course, although I was mad as fire at the time.' His expression became grave. 'I said some horrible things to you in the heat of my anger. Can you bring yourself to forgive me, Fliss?'

'Of course I can,' she said, quickly getting up and hugging him. Eventually, after they had released one another, she said to him, 'Does your friend give any other news, or is it all private?' She wanted very badly to broach the subject of Melissa and Octavius, but did not know how much Richard knew.

'No, no, not at all,' he said, finding his place on the page. 'He writes "send my good wishes to all your family. I do so miss you all in Bath. It's doubly dull with Nick gone too, whether to London or abroad again, I don't know. Anyway, I am consoling myself with a charming lady who came to Bath the day after you left . . ."'

They heard a tiny gasp and, looking round, they saw Melissa, looking paler than ever and holding on to the door frame for support. She took a step or two forward, put out one hand, and then fainted. They both hurried to her side.

'I was afraid something like this might happen,' said Fliss in worried tones. 'She has been looking unwell since we got back from Bath. Will you carry her upstairs please, Richard?'

Richard picked her up in his arms, saying as he did so, 'You're right, Fliss. She's a mere featherweight. She can't have been eating properly.'

Once he had laid her down on the bed that she and Fliss shared, Fliss said to him, 'Melissa was supposed to be teaching the younger ones. Would you mind going to see what they are doing? I will look after her now.' There was some water in a pitcher on a cupboard near the window. Fliss poured some into a glass then dampened a handkerchief in the pitcher and used it to wipe Melissa's face. The young woman soon began to come round and, after she had sat up and taken a few sips of water, she was starting to look more like her normal self, although still rather pale.

'I'm sorry, Fliss,' she said, with a weak attempt at a smile. 'I hope I didn't worry you too much.'

'You did give us rather a scare,' admitted Fliss. 'Not but what I have been half expecting it to happen anyway. You're not looking well, Lissa.' Her sister looked away and said nothing, so Fliss went on gently, 'Is it Mama's death, or is it something else that has distressed you and is making you starve yourself? You really need to take more nourishment, or you will never get back to normal.'

'Normal?' said Melissa with a humourless laugh. 'Don't you understand, Fliss, that nothing will ever be normal again?'

'Lissa?' said Fliss uncomprehendingly. 'What do you mean?'

'You might as well know now as later,' said her sister wearily. 'Fliss, I'm with child.'

CHAPTER FOURTEEN

Fliss stared at her sister in horrified silence. It was Melissa who spoke first.

'You're the one we all depend on, Fliss. You put us all right, don't you? Well, mend that if you can.' She spoke in a cynical tone, but there was a tiny fragment of something in her voice which seemed to suggest that she had some small hope that her sister might be able to help her, even in this situation.

'Lissa, are you sure?' Fliss said at last.

'Yes, quite sure. You know that my courses are never late.'

'Does he know?' Melissa shook her head.

'Do you remember that I went out the day we left Bath? I went to find him. Of course, I was not sure then, just . . . just suspicious, but I wanted to see him, to tell him where I was going, and why. I discovered that he had gone to Bristol to look at a horse. I left a message with Ruth Stringer, but I have heard nothing. Fliss, I don't know where he is. Surely, if he cared for me he would come! But in that letter that Richard read out . . . Oh, what shall I tell Papa and the rest of them?' Panic started to rise in her voice and Fliss took hold of her hands.

'I know this is difficult for you, Lissa, but we'll find a way through, I promise. We don't need to tell Papa yet. The first thing to do is to tell Octavius. We know he is still in Bath, so Richard can take a letter and be sure that he will receive it. It is only right that he should be told, after all.'

'Octavius?' said Lissa with a puzzled expression on her face.

'Yes, Octavius; the father of your child.'

There was a short silence, then Melissa said in a low voice, 'Octavius is not the father of my child.'

'Then who?' asked Fliss. She had been so convinced that her sister was enamoured of the handsome young officer, that she was unable to imagine who else it might be.

'It's Nick.'

'Lord Nick Bonsor?' whispered Fliss, astonished. Lissa bowed her head. Fliss closed her eyes for a moment, remembering his lordship's dissipated face, his outrageous flirting, his tarnished reputation. Of course, it was far more plausible that he should be the father rather than Octavius. Sadly enough, though, it was also very unlikely that such a man would be prepared to make an honourable gesture towards a woman he had wronged. Suddenly a thought occurred to her.

'But Lissa, you barely know him,' she said.

Melissa smiled faintly. 'I've known him for a long time. I met him in London, two years ago.' They were both silent for a short time, then Melissa went on, 'I never told you much about my London season, did I?'

Fliss shook her head. 'I always assumed that because you had only a small portion, you had a very limited success, and therefore you didn't want to talk about it much.'

'Limited?' Melissa laughed bitterly. 'I was an utter failure. There are plenty of pretty girls with respectable fortunes to attract suitors, and a penniless girl with no noble connections has very little chance. Despite my godmother's best efforts I spent the first three weeks being almost completely ignored. It was horrible, Fliss. Horrible! People staring at you, weighing you up and finding you wanting.

'Then Nick came. I can't begin to tell you what a difference he made to me. He had been out of town, and when he returned, the first thing that he did was go to the theatre. I was sitting in Aunt Rose's box, waiting for the play to begin. We were on our own as usual, save for Aunt's cousin Henry and his wife. Then all at once, I felt someone's eyes upon me, and turning my head, I saw Nick looking at me from another box. He sketched an outrageously flirtatious bow at me, and of course I looked away at once, but I could not help peeping at him, although I tried hard not to do so. Before the farce, he left his box and came round to be introduced to me.

'After that evening, he began to seek me out. He was obviously attracted to me and I was lonely and tired of being overlooked, but I

196

soon realized that my life had changed. Nick's reputation is appalling, but he is seen as being an arbiter of female beauty. My lack of fortune was still a problem, but I began to attract a small group of admirers and I think that at that stage, had I shown myself interested, I might have received an offer. Unfortunately, however, the damage was done. I had fallen in love with Nick, even though I knew that to him I was just an amusing diversion. I left London with no suitor, a broken heart, and the knowledge that I had given my affection to a man who did not care a straw for me. Of course, I did not hear from him.'

'I always wondered why you were so quiet,' said Fliss. 'I thought that it was simply because you had not come back engaged as everyone had hoped.'

'It was partly that, but it was chiefly because I couldn't stop thinking of Nick,' admitted Melissa. 'Then we went to Bath and I met him again.'

'So that day in the Pump Room, when you felt dizzy, it was not because you saw Octavius, but because you had seen Nick,' exclaimed Fliss.

'That's right,' replied Melissa. 'Once we were able to talk to one another, it was as if we had never been apart. And he seemed different; gentler somehow.' She looked down at her hands, then back up at her sister again. 'I'm sorry to have deceived you, Fliss, but you

197

made it so easy for me by thinking I was interested in Octavius.'

'And I suppose that all those times when you were supposed to be with Ruth Stringer . . .'

'I was with Nick. Yes, mostly.'

'And when I saw you coming out of Edgar Buildings that day with Octavius . . .'

Melissa lifted her head then. 'No, I was telling you the truth. On that occasion, I really had been visiting Richard, because I was worried about him. But I did deliberately mislead you, because I swore that I had not visited Octavius in his lodgings, but I had been there before, only with Nick.'

Fliss, who had managed to keep calm until now, suddenly felt her anger boil over and she exclaimed, 'Lissa, how could you?'

Melissa looked her straight in the eye. 'I've already told you—I love him. Don't run away with the idea that he was entirely to blame. I wanted him just as much as he wanted me.' Then her face crumpled and she cried, 'Oh Fliss, why hasn't he come?'

With that Fliss's anger evaporated. She put her arms round her sister. Melissa had made a mistake but it looked as if she would spend the rest of her life paying for it. Having her own suspicions about why Lord Nick had failed to appear, Fliss said merely, 'Are you sure that he will have received your message?'

'He must have done! The Stringers were certainly fixed in Bath for some time and I

know that Ruth will have passed it on because
. . .'

'Because?' prompted Fliss gently.

'Because she thought it excessively romantic
that I should be in love with a rake,'
murmured Melissa. 'Fliss, he isn't going to
come, is he?'

Fliss could not bring herself to lie, but she
said simply, 'I don't know, Lissa. All kinds of
things might have happened to prevent him
from receiving your message, or from coming
even if he did receive it. Have you written
again to Ruth Stringer?'

'Yes,' admitted Melissa. 'I wrote to her over
a week ago, and I have heard nothing. But
remember what was in Richard's letter: if
Octavius does not know the whereabouts of his
own brother, is it likely that Ruth Stringer will
know? Besides . . .'

'Yes?' prompted Fliss again.

'I'm not at all sure that in ordinary
circumstances either one of us would choose
to keep in contact with the other.'

Fliss thought for a moment. 'Did you tell
her that you were with child?' she asked
eventually.

Lissa shook her head. 'I haven't told anyone
except for you. It is only in this last week that I
have been absolutely sure. In any case, I
suppose I thought that if I told someone it
would make it more real, more final. And it
has.' She shivered and Fliss hugged her.

199

'I'm glad you've told me,' she said. 'We'll give Ruth Stringer another week to reply. If you have not heard by then, we will try to think of some other way in which to proceed.'

They waited for a week, but the only letter that arrived was one for Fliss from James, telling her that although his business in Lincolnshire was finished, he had gone down to London to meet William there. Obviously Ruth either could not or would not answer. Eventually, Fliss raised the subject with her sister again.

'Lissa, what can we do? We cannot keep your condition a secret for ever.' Lissa got up and walked across the room. She was reed slim, and Fliss was still anxious about her lack of appetite.

'I don't know, Fliss. Perhaps I could go away somewhere?'

'To have the baby and . . .'

'To have the baby and keep it,' said Melissa firmly. 'Can you imagine that I would ever give up Nick's child?' Fliss did not comment on this. Both of them knew all too well that there was nowhere for her to go. Only one way of doing it occurred to her. There still remained £400 from her portion. It might serve to keep Lissa hidden and provided for, if she lived frugally, until she could claim her own money, but it would be a bleak existence.

'I have an idea,' said Fliss at last. 'Lissa, do I have your permission to seek a solution—if I can?'

'I suppose so. As long as it doesn't mean telling Papa.'

'Lissa, he'll have to know some time . . .'

'No!' cried Lissa, her voice rising almost on a note of hysteria. 'Please not yet!' Her face crumpled. 'Oh Fliss, if only Mama were here.' As she cradled her sobbing sister, Fliss found herself wishing the same thing most profoundly.

'Try not to become too distressed,' she murmured against her sister's hair. 'I'll never desert you; I swear it.'

In all truth, the solution that Fliss had in mind did not involve speaking to her father. He still showed no signs of taking any interest in his family, and spent a good deal of time shut away in his study. Richard had returned to Bath at Fliss's urging. Only that day, they had had a letter from him which said that on hearing from Mrs Salisbury that Sir James had gone to London he had decided to go there, too, to discuss his possible diplomatic future. Even had he not gone, Fliss doubted whether she would have confided in him. His hopes of marrying Alice would surely be compromised by the intelligence that his beloved's uncle had seduced his sister. The one man to whom she would have been tempted to turn had gone to London, and she could not approach him because he was a close friend of Nick. Nevertheless, for very different reasons it was to London that Fliss decided to go. If Lord Nick was to be a father, then someone ought to inform him of the fact. She was convinced that he would not be prepared to marry Melissa, but it might be possible to persuade him to contribute to the upkeep of his child.

From Octavius's letter, it was clear that Nick was no longer in Bath. He had only just returned from the Continent; the Bonsor family did not seem to be particularly close, so he would probably not have gone to Brigham. The most likely thing, therefore, was that he would have gone to London. Once in London, if Nick's whereabouts were not immediately obvious, she could always go to Sir James's house in Grosvenor Square and ask him for his help, making up some pretext if necessary. The problem was how to get there. She really needed a male escort, but it had to be someone whose discretion could be relied upon.

After the family meal, she wandered outside in order to think hard about how it could be managed. She had dismissed the possibility of going to London in male attire because she was too short and her curves were far too feminine for her to be able to borrow any of her brothers' clothes. Slowly she walked along the gravel drive, praying for inspiration, and just as she drew close to the box hedge, someone stepped out from the shadows, startling her so much that she would have screamed had the figure not covered her mouth with a gloved hand.

'It's all right,' whispered the unmistakable voice of her brother Christopher. 'It's only me.'

'What are you doing here?' she asked him, as soon as he had uncovered her mouth. 'You should be at Cambridge.' Even while she was speaking, the glimmering of an idea was coming into her mind.

'I'm very sorry, Fliss, but I'm afraid I've been sent down. You see, I . . .' It was at this point that his sensible sister surprised him more than she had ever done in the whole of his life.

'Splendid!' she declared. 'In that case, you can take me to London!'

CHAPTER FIFTEEN

It was surprisingly easy to persuade Christopher to fall in with her plan. Before he had time to question her, she bustled him inside the house and into the bookroom. Once there, he exclaimed, 'London! But why on earth would you want to go to London?'

'Believe me, Chris, it is important. If I could tell you, then I would, but it is not my secret.' Then she added, 'I promise I'll make everything right with Papa.' They both spoke in hushed tones, as if they were involved in some kind of conspiracy.

Christopher needed no further urging. He went that very evening to the inn in the village, judging that the landlord would be likely to be well informed about when and where to catch the mail coach, and he came back big with news.

'The passengers on the mail stay the night at Marlborough,' he said excitedly. 'If we go there tonight, we could catch it there.'

'Tonight!' exclaimed Fliss.

'Well, you want to go, don't you?' Suddenly it seemed as if Chris were the instigator, and she the follower.

'Of course! But Chris, how can we be sure that we will get seats? They might all be taken.'

'Yes they might. The landlord said he thought it unlikely. Most of the traffic will be in the other direction, the London season not having started properly yet. I can go to Bath, if you like, and book places for us, but it will take longer. What do you want me to do?'

Fliss thought for a moment then said, 'We'll go to Marlborough. It is not far, and if the coach is full we'll be no worse off. We'll decide what to do in those circumstances if necessary.'

'It must be very urgent,' said Chris.

'Yes, it is, but I can't say any more. I'm sorry, Chris. Have you eaten, by the way?'

'Yes, I stopped by the Thorntons' farm and

had some bread and cheese with them. I thought you'd have eaten here, and I wanted to tell Jed about why I'd been sent down. He won't give me away.' Jed Thornton, the family's eldest son, was the same age as Chris and the two had played together as boys.

'You can tell me all about it later,' she promised. 'But for now, let's go upstairs and get ready. Try to keep out of sight; the fewer people who know about your presence here, the better.' They safely negotiated the stairs and the passage without being seen, and soon Christopher was safely installed in the room that he shared with Richard. 'Richard is away just now, so no one will come in,' Fliss explained. 'Now don't move; I'll go and get Barbara.'

As the family kept country hours, it was still only eight o'clock, but all the younger ones were already safely tucked up in bed. Mr Wintershill did not encourage the family to linger downstairs after dinner, and those who did so felt no inclination to chatter and laugh when he was shut away in his study close by. Consequently, the social hub of the house tended to be the schoolroom, and it was there that Fliss found Barbara, Elizabeth and Susan. Walter and Wilfred had returned to school after the funeral.

As soon as they had left the schoolroom, Fliss said to her sister, 'Where's Lissa?'

'She's in the nursery with Nanny,' replied

Barbara. 'Oh Fliss, she doesn't look at all well, does she? What are we going to do?'

'I'll tell you as much as I can in a minute,' she said. 'But for now come to the boys' room, and don't make a fuss when you see who's there.' Needless to say, Barbara was delighted to see her twin, and Fliss had to be patient whilst they hugged each other enthusiastically. But when Barbara wanted Chris to tell her the story of his being sent down, Fliss called a halt.

'Not just now, there's a lot to do,' she said. 'Babs, you're going to have to hold the fort again for a little while. Chris and I are driving to Marlborough tonight and if all goes well we intend to catch the mail coach to London.'

'London!' exclaimed Barbara. 'But why?'

Fliss took a deep breath. 'You were asking me about Lissa and what we could do just now. Well, it is on Lissa's account that I'm going. I'm afraid I can't tell you any more than that.'

'Are you going to fetch a doctor?' asked Barbara.

Fliss smiled. 'Perhaps,' she said.

'But what are you going to tell Papa?'

'I've thought about that,' replied Fliss. 'I think I shall tell him that Sir James's aunt has been taken ill. In view of her recent kindness to me and Melissa, it will not be surprising if I feel it to be my duty to go and be with her.'

The twins looked at one another for a moment, then, displaying the unspoken communication which took place so often between them that the rest of the family took it for granted, Christopher said, 'We think that you ought to let Barbara tell Papa in the morning.'

'Why?' asked Fliss.

'I'm better at lying than you are,' said Barbara frankly.

'All right then,' conceded Fliss. 'I agree that I'm quite hopeless at concealing anything.'

'What about Melissa?' asked Barbara. 'Do you want me to tell her the same story?'

'No; I'll do that. If I do not come to our room tonight she will be anxious and think it strange that I have not spoken to her. I'll go to the nursery and see her now.'

When Fliss got to the nursery, however, she found that Lissa had fallen asleep on the truckle bed which was always kept in there and which Nanny used if any of the children was unwell.

'Poor mite,' whispered Nanny when Fliss came in. 'She's worn out; well, it's not surprising in her condition.' She looked at Fliss and their glances met in a moment of complete understanding. 'What's to be done for her?'

'I'm going to do what I can,' replied Fliss. 'But not a word to Lissa. My plans may come to nothing.' She walked to the door and was about to leave when Nanny said, 'Bring him back with you if you can; that'll be the best medicine.' Fliss did not ask Nanny to keep her knowledge of Lissa's condition to herself. Their secrets had always been safe with Nanny.

She went to her room to discover that the efficient Barbara had already packed for her.

'Thank you Babs, you're wonderful,' she said, hugging her. 'Lissa is asleep in the nursery with Nanny so I haven't told her anything. You can tell her the same story as Papa in the morning.'

'Just come back soon, with help for Lissa if you can,' Barbara replied.

It was a fine evening with a full moon, and it was a very easy matter for Christopher to drive them to Marlborough in the old gig. As they left the drive, Fliss glanced over in the direction of Roache Hall. How she would have liked to have confided in James and gone to him for help. Perhaps, though, it was just as well. She had no way of knowing how he would take the news that Nick had made Melissa pregnant and, much though she loved James, she could not be sure of the rightness of telling him what Melissa had told her in confidence. It was probably true also that James, unlike Chris, would not have been prepared to take her to London without being told why.

The landlord at the King's Head in Marlborough had not filled all his rooms, and he was very glad to have two extra guests. It was here that the passengers of the London mail stayed the night, and their host was obliging enough to call the guard through in order to ask him whether there were any places. The guard looked regretful.

'I can fit you inside, ma'am,' he said to Fliss, 'but the young gentleman will have to travel on top as there is only space for one more passenger in the coach.' Fliss looked at her younger brother, who seemed rather pleased than otherwise.

'We'll take the places you have,' said Fliss, counting out the correct money and reflecting that with Chris travelling on the roof, that would at least mean a saving in the fare! That being settled, the landlord showed them to their rooms, promising to make sure that they were roused at half past seven the following morning, so as to be in time to take breakfast and board the mail.

Once alone, Fliss prepared for bed. It was the first time that she had stayed in an inn without an older relative. The knowledge of Christopher's presence in the next room was reassuring, and the familiar sight of her own hairbrush and comb on the table by the window comforted her a little. Once in bed, she sat up, her arms clasped around her knees, and began to review the task ahead of her.

When or how the idea of seeking out Lord Nick had come to her she could not say. If she were honest with herself, she would have to say that she was not optimistic about the chances of his renouncing his wild behaviour and becoming a model husband. There came into her mind the memory of how he had said that declaring the world well lost for love was not a sensible course. That attitude hardly argued a willingness to marry a penniless girl.

On the other hand, although he was undoubtedly a rake, she had noticed some kindly traits in him—but witness his going with James on the night of the elopement for no other discernible reason than because Alice would need someone. Whatever might be Nick's reaction to the news that he was to be a father, Fliss was convinced that he should be told. She realized that part of the reason why she would not have wanted to tell James about Melissa's baby was that she felt that Nick had a right to be the first to know.

She lay down, closed her eyes, and started to wonder how she would go about finding Nick when they got to London. She knew that Sir James lived in Grosvenor Square, and if all else failed she could go there and ask him where she might find Nick. She was in the middle of an imaginary and very convoluted conversation with James in which, without mentioning Melissa, she was trying to give a convincing explanation of why she had come to London in order to seek out one of its most notorious libertines, when she fell asleep.

She was woken by the sound of knocking on the door and a reminder that the mail would be leaving in an hour. Her tangled thoughts had meant that she had slept fitfully, and consequently did not feel very rested, but splashing her face with cold water from the ewer refreshed her a little. A look at Christopher's healthy complexion downstairs told her that the disgrace of being sent down and the excitement of going to London had disturbed his slumbers not at all.

'I say, Fliss, this is famous sport,' he said to her, his face glowing, before he clambered up on to the roof. Fliss could not help but smile at his enthusiasm, despite the serious nature of their mission, and she took her place inside.

As she was the last to join the party, she was sitting with her back to the horses, but she was a good traveller and did not mind. Opposite her was a respectable-looking married couple, who said very little to one another, and between them sat their daughter, a child of about twelve. Sitting next to Fliss was a doctor, who spent nearly the whole time with his nose in a book.

Most of the time, Fliss occupied herself with looking out of the window at the passing scenery, and as this was a completely new journey to her, she found much to interest her. They stopped at Speenhamland at The Pelican for lunch, and there they changed horses for the second time. By now, Fliss was very glad to talk to Chris, for she had become a little tired of sitting in silence.

'It's just as good as I thought it would be,'

he declared, his enthusiasm undiminished. 'You can see so much from up there—things that I daresay you missed, being inside. I was hoping that the coachman would let me take a turn with the ribbons, but he wouldn't hear of it,' he added regretfully.

'I should think not, when the mail is being carried!' replied Fliss.

The rest of the day's journey passed as uneventfully as the first part. Even Maidenhead Thicket, a notorious haunt for highwaymen, was traversed safely, and the party was soon comfortably installed at The Crown for the night. It was here that the doctor ended his journey and, as no one else was to board the coach, this meant that Christopher could travel inside. At first inclined to reject the idea, he became more reconciled to it when the morning dawned grey and cloudy. Sure enough it had started to rain before they reached Slough and he had to admit that he was very glad to be inside.

The rain continued unremitting for the rest of their journey, and making it difficult to see anything outside the coach. Fliss was thankful for Christopher's company, and they beguiled the journey by chatting idly about family concerns. She also told him something about the time that she and Melissa had spent in Bath, but since for various reasons, she was reluctant to say very much about Nick, Richard and Alice, or even James, her account

212

was a little sparse.

Christopher evidently thought so, for when she fell silent, he said, 'I'd have thought that you'd have more to say about James.'

'Why should I?' she asked, trying to make her voice sound natural.

'Well, he was there for practically the whole time that you were,' replied Christopher, matter-of-factly.

'Nonsense,' said Fliss blushing. 'Anyway, I do not see how you could possibly know as you weren't there.'

'Barbara told me. She said that he only came back to Roache Hall when he had to, then he was off to Bath again as fast as he could go. Don't tell me that was to see his aunt! If you ask me, he's sweet on you.'

'Nonsense,' said Fliss again. She glanced across at the woman opposite, who was glaring at her as if she were some kind of temptress.

At last they reached journey's end at the Bell Savage on Ludgate Hill. They got down from the coach, the married woman carefully drawing her husband away from Fliss's wicked presence.

'Did you see that?' asked Christopher, his eyes sparkling. 'She thought you were some sort of Jezebel! What a joke!'

'It is nothing of the sort,' said Fliss indignantly. 'Keep your voice down, you dreadful boy, or I shall have no reputation left! Listen Chris, I had not given any thought to where we might stay in London.'

'We could stay here,' suggested her brother. 'It's a respectable inn, if rather busy.' Fliss looked round. They could certainly waste a lot of time and money looking for somewhere else. While she hesitated, Christopher pointed to a gentleman who was obviously a guest and said, 'Look, there is a clergyman staying here! What could be more respectable than that?'

Fliss smiled, but said, 'Very well then, it is decided. Arrange for rooms will you please, Chris? And find out whether we can dine here. Oh, and tell the landlord that we are not sure for how long we shall be staying.'

Christopher paused for a moment, then said, 'Anything else?'

Fliss shook her head. Now that they were in London, the enormity of her task was beginning to hit home. Once they were settled in, she would have to take Christopher into her confidence, at least to some degree. She was going to need some help.

There proved to be no difficulty in reserving rooms for a few nights, and the landlord did not need to know in advance for how long they would be staying. He also assured them that they would be able to eat at the inn if they so wished. With all that arranged, Fliss began to feel a little more optimistic. True, they were no nearer their goal, but at least they had a base.

Having been sitting for most of the last two

214

days, they both felt in need of a walk, so they wandered along to St Paul's to have a look around. Fliss had never seen such a great building in her life, and wanted to spend some considerable time admiring it. She fully expected Christopher to tire of looking round very quickly, but to her surprise, he was very well informed about the building and about Sir Christopher Wren, and he talked very knowledgeably about buildings, their design and the best materials to use.

'Why Chris, I do believe you would like to design buildings yourself,' she declared in surprise.

'There's nothing I'd like better,' he responded frankly. 'What I would really like to do would be to go abroad and see for myself how buildings are designed and constructed, particularly in Italy. But I can't see that happening.'

His words reminded Fliss of the precarious financial state of the family, and of the need to regularize Melissa's affairs.

'Chris, I want to tell you a little about what I'm doing in London, because I'm going to need your help,' she said. 'Tomorrow, we must set about finding Lord Nick Bonsor.'

'Lord Nick!' he exclaimed. 'You mean, the disreputable older brother of Richard's friend Octavius?'

'Yes,' replied Fliss.

'But why? How? Where?'

'As to why, I cannot tell you, except that it is very important. As to where, well, I have been thinking, Chris. Gentlemen go to clubs, don't they? You are a gentleman. You can go and seek him out, and when you have found him, you can tell him where we are staying, and arrange for him to come and meet me at the Bell Savage.'

Christopher looked horror-struck. 'But I've never met him, Fliss,' he protested.

'That's easy; he looks exactly like an older version of his brother, Lord Octavius,' she answered reassuringly.

'That's no good; I haven't met him either. Remember that Richard and his friend had left by the time I arrived from Cambridge.'

Fliss looked at him in nonplussed silence, before saying, with a confidence that she was far from feeling, 'Well then, you must just ask someone to point him out.'

'But Fliss, I can't!' he said anxiously. 'I'm not a member of any clubs. You can't just walk into them off the street and demand an entrance, you know. At least,' he qualified carefully, 'you may be able to do so with some of them but I don't know which ones. And there are dozens of gentlemen's clubs in London. I might go into twenty and not find him!' Fliss looked at her brother. He had done so much for her—she could never have managed to get to London without him—but he was still only eighteen.

'Well what shall we do then?' she asked him.

'We could go into the fashionable part of town tomorrow, and walk up and down and see if we can see him,' suggested Christopher.

'Yes, and we could end up just missing him all day,' retorted Fliss.

'There is one other thing we could do,' said Christopher tentatively after a long silence.

'Well?'

'Well . . . didn't you tell me that Sir James is in London?' he ventured. 'We could seek him out. He might know where to find Lord Nick.' There was another long silence.

'We'll try your other plan first,' said Fliss eventually. 'Come on, let's go back to the inn. We've just got time to change before dinner.'

The food at the Bell Savage was excellent and Fliss and Christopher were very glad that they had chosen to stay there. The clergyman, whom Christopher had noticed, was indeed staying at the inn and he proved to be a Mr Woodforde from East Anglia. In conversation with him, they discovered that he had moved to the Bell Savage from the Swan and Two Necks in Lad Lane because he did not like it, and was very pleased with his decision.

The following morning, they were up in good time, chiefly, as Fliss remarked at the breakfast-table, because they had neither of them slept well.

'What a noisy place London is to be sure,' she declared to the innkeeper. 'Does nobody

217

ever sleep?'

'It took me ages to drop off, and then it only seemed to be five minutes later that some fellow outside told me what time it was and woke me up again,' added Christopher. 'I nearly threw something out of the window at him, I can tell you!'

The innkeeper, whose name was Barton, smiled civilly. 'It's just a question of what you're used to, ma'am and sir,' he said. 'I visited my cousins in the country once. They have a farm out Maidenhead way. I couldn't sleep a wink all night, it was so quiet!'

'That's probably true,' agreed Fliss, then looked meaningly at Christopher until he said, 'Oh yes, I was going to ask you, Landlord, if you could procure us a hackney? We want to see the fashionable sights.'

'By all means,' replied Barton. 'Just tell me when you're ready and I'll send a lad out to get one for you.'

By the time they had breakfasted and made themselves ready, the morning was well advanced, and their journey in the hackney through the crowded streets took some time. So absorbed were they in all the sights that they were amazed when they were set down in New Bond Street and discovered that it was already noon. It was clearly a popular promenade for the ton, for fashionably dressed men and women were strolling up and down.

Fliss looked down at her mourning black in

dismay, then squared her shoulders and said, 'Come on, Chris. The sooner we start, the more likely we are to find him.'

Christopher felt quite as self-conscious as she, but he had just as much pride, and together they negotiated the fashionable parade, trying to ignore the occasional contemptuous stare. They turned off New Bond Street and walked up one side of Conduit Street and down the other, then turning back into New Bond Street, they walked along it until they reached Oxford Street. At any other time, Fliss would have thoroughly enjoyed the sights and sounds, and the variety of shops in particular, but she was too busy looking for Nick Bonsor to be able to give her attention to anything other than the many people who were obviously out just to see and be seen.

They walked a little way along Oxford Street, then retraced their steps until they were back at the bottom of New Bond Street again. After they had negotiated their route for the fourth time, however, and failed to see Nick Bonsor, or indeed anyone resembling him, Christopher said, 'This is no good, Fliss. Come on, let's see if we can find refreshment somewhere, and then decide what to do next.' Fliss readily agreed, so they turned off Bond Street, having no idea where to go, but keeping to streets that appeared to be well frequented and quite fashionable. After a short time, more by luck than good judgement, they found themselves in Berkeley Square.

'Look, Gunther's!' exclaimed Fliss. 'I heard Melissa speak of it. We'll be able to get some refreshments there.' But when they reached the famous pastry-cook's, their courage deserted them, for the place was full of just the same kind of people who had looked so contemptuously at them in Bond Street.

'Come along,' said Christopher. 'I've got an idea! I think I know the way to St James's Park from here, and I'm told you can buy milk which has been drawn straight from the cow.'

Christopher proved to be a reliable guide, and after they had reached the park, drunk a refreshing glass of milk, and sat on a bench for a time, they both felt a lot better.

'What now?' said Christopher eventually.

'I don't know,' replied Fliss. 'We could spend years doing what we've done this morning and still not find him.'

'Do you know what I think?' said Chris. Fliss said nothing, but she knew exactly what he was going to say. 'I think you should go and ask Sir James.' Still she said nothing. 'Fliss, why are you so reluctant to go and see him? He is the only person we know well in London. He will help us, I'm sure.'

'Yes. Yes, of course you're right,' she said. She stood up and brushed down her skirt. 'Let's go then.'

'Now?' asked Christopher.

'Well, you know what the bard says: "If 'twere done when 'tis done, then 'twere well it were done quickly". Come on.'

CHAPTER SIXTEEN

Fliss could not have explained to Christopher why exactly she did not want to go to James for help. There was, of course, the fact that she did not want to have to tell him about Melissa, but there were other reasons. She had not spoken to him since her mother's funeral and, on that occasion, he had called her 'my dear' and had seemed about to say something important. Over two weeks had passed since then, however, and she had had only one letter from him in which he had written no words of love. Furthermore, she had had time to remember Mrs Grantham, and about how many people seemed to think that he and the handsome widow would make a match of it. True, Christopher had thought that James had gone to Bath in pursuit of her, but he might not have been aware that he had brought Mrs Grantham with him.

Fliss thought back to the time when she and James had kissed in the Sydney Gardens. She had known at the time that she was in love with him, which perhaps excused her conduct, but he had not made any avowals of affection to her. She reminded herself that though reformed, James had himself been a rake, and perhaps some of those tendencies remained.

She was going to find it difficult with all these jumbled thoughts to confront James, and she found herself hoping, as they drew near to Grosvenor Square, that he would not be at home. As they entered the square, they both gazed around them in amazement.

'I had not expected it to be so huge,' said Christopher.

'Neither did I,' agreed Fliss. 'We shall never find James's house. Come on, let's go back to the Bell Savage.' But Christopher, now that they were within sight of their goal, proved to be made of sterner stuff. Beckoning over a boy who looked as if he might be a kitchen lad on an errand, he held out a coin.

'Here, this is for you if you can tell us where Sir James Singleton lives.'

'Over there,' said the boy pointing to a house quite close to where they were standing. 'That one with the blue door.'

'Do you want me to come in with you?' asked Christopher. Fliss shook her head.

'Wait and see if he is in. If so, can you come back for me in half an hour?' Christopher gave her hand a little squeeze.

'Of course I will,' he replied, then added, 'I don't know what you're so nervous about. Anyone would have supposed that he might have grown an extra head whilst in town, the way that you're behaving.' They approached the front door and knocked on it. Had it been a servant who had never been to Roache Hall, they might have found it difficult to gain an entrance, unfashionably dressed as they were. Fortunately, however, the footman who opened the door had been with the household to the country on more than one occasion and he recognized them immediately.

'Good day,' said Fliss, her voice full of confidence, none of which she was feeling. 'Is Sir James within?' The footman, well trained though he was, betrayed a moment's hesitation.

'He is here, Miss Wintershill,' he said doubtfully, 'but I fear that he is a trifle . . . unwell.'

'Unwell? In what way? Has the doctor been?' asked Fliss anxiously.

'Well . . .'

Here, Christopher astonished all present, including himself, by saying in a forthright manner, 'Well, my man, are you going to admit my sister, or is it the custom in Grosvenor Square to keep ladies standing on the doorstep?' The footman made haste to apologize and stepped back to let Fliss in. 'I'll be back in half an hour,' promised Christopher.

Once she was inside, it occurred to Fliss that she had put herself into an extremely compromising position. She had criticized

223

Melissa for visiting Richard in his apartments in Bath, but what she was doing now was infinitely worse. She had never even visited Roache Hall alone, and this was London, where a woman was expected to be far more circumspect in her conduct. If James was thinking of resuming his previous rakish behaviour, her appearance unchaperoned would do anything but discourage him. Suddenly she realized that whilst she was standing in a state of indecision, the footman was behaving in a similar way and, taking a leaf out of her brother's book, she drew herself up, and said, 'Show me to your master if you please.'

The footman did not take her upstairs, as she had expected, but to a downstairs room, opened the door, announced her and withdrew. She stood just inside the room looking at James as she had never seen him before. Early as it was, he was quite obviously drunk. In his right hand he was holding a wine bottle, and in his left, he had an empty glass. He had discarded his coat and cravat, his waistcoat hung open and his shirt was unfastened at the neck. His hair was hanging loose upon his shoulders, his chin was unshaven, his linen seemed somewhat rumpled and altogether, he looked every inch the disreputable rake that he had claimed to be in Bath.

'Felicity my dear!' he exclaimed, raising his

glass to her. 'This is a pleasant surprise. You are just in time to help me finish the bottle.' He wandered over to the sideboard where there was another glass and poured wine into it and into his own, slopping it over the sideboard as he did so. 'Now tell me—in what way may I'—he hiccoughed—'serve you?' Fliss looked at him in dismay. She had never seen anyone in quite this condition before. Richard had occasionally become a little giggly on special occasions, and then he had been hustled straight to bed. She had never witnessed anyone with such a reckless glitter in his eye as James was displaying.

'I . . . I—it doesn't matter,' she said. 'I . . . I think I'd better go.'

'Go? But you've only just arrived! Come! Don't stand there by the door, take off your bonnet and come and join me in a glass of wine! Can't you see that this is a celebration?'

'Celebration?' asked Fliss, puzzled. She took off her cloak and bonnet and laid them on a chair by the door. She then took the glass of wine that he offered her, but resolved to take only small sips, for he was standing close by with the bottle still in his hand, and she was afraid that he might pour her some more at the slightest opportunity.

'Why certainly,' he replied, going back to the sideboard to pick up his own glass. 'I'm a very lucky man, Felicity. Did you know that? A lucky man. Sit down and I'll tell you about it.'

Fliss said nothing, but sat down cautiously on the edge of a chair. She was not afraid of James, but she had no way of knowing how a man in his condition might react if she did not comply with his wishes. 'Not curious?' he went on. 'How strange! Most of your sex are incurab . . . incurab . . . extremely curious.' He laughed at his own difficulty with the words.

'If I can help with anything . . .' began Fliss cautiously.

'Oh, help! Yes, you're very good at that, aren't you, Felicity? Everybody leans on you, don't they? Do you like that, Felicity? Being important and essential to everybody?'

'No, I . . . well, it just . . . happened.'

'It just happened, did it? Do you know what I think? I think that your family is like a vampire, Felicity. They're sucking you dry. And the worst of it is, you enjoy it.' Indignant then, she made as if to get up in protest, but James moved closer, looming over her so that she shrank back before the hint of menace in his gaze. 'Well Miss Problem-solver, would you like to see whether you can sort out my little problem? Will you enjoy that?'

Now hardly seemed to be the time to say that she had come to him because she had a problem of her own, so she said hesitantly, 'I . . . I will help if I can.'

'Oh, I doubt if this is within your power to repair,' he said. 'Do you remember why I came to London?'

226

'To see William, was it not?' she replied.

'Yes, William, my son . . . my son . . .' His voice broke a little as he repeated the words.

'Oh James, no!' she exclaimed, in sudden horror. 'He is not . . . ?'

'Not dead, I think you were going to say. No, he is not dead, but he might as well be.'

'What do you mean? Is he ill? Is he here in London?'

'No, he is not ill; no, he is not in London; at least, not any more. He is on his way back to Rome. My son, Felicity, has decided to become a priest.'

'A priest?'

'And not only a priest, but a priest in the church of Rome!' As if it had only just dawned upon him, he turned and hurled his glass into the grate, surprising Fliss so much that she sprang up out of her chair. He stood staring down at the shards for a few moments then turned back to face her. 'I sent him abroad to complete his education, you know? Other men's sons go abroad, amuse themselves with foreign women, and come back with a lot of useless statuary and bad paintings. My son comes back with a calling!' So saying, he dropped the bottle, threw himself into a chair and sat with his head in his hands.

Fliss stood looking at him for a time, then ventured to say, 'His decision is final, then?'

'Oh yes, his decision is final. He is not quite twenty-one so I could forbid him, but what

227

would be the point?' He laughed bitterly. 'He thought about it and discussed it with some priests he met in Rome, with someone he stayed with, with someone he met on his journey, with almost anyone except for me, in fact.'

'Perhaps he was afraid of what you might say or do,' ventured Fliss.

'Afraid? He might well be! How did he think I would react when I discovered that he plans to throw away everything that I have worked to pass on to him?'

Fliss waited for a moment, then said cautiously, 'You said he is no longer in London.'

He looked up at her. 'That's right.' He turned his face away from her. 'I threw him out.'

'You threw him out!' she exclaimed. 'But James, he is your son.'

'My son!' he said bitterly. 'My son has a duty to pass on my name.'

'Yes, but suppose this had not happened. He might never have married. Some men do not. Nick Bonsor has not. Or if he had married, he might have had no children, or only had daughters.'

'That would have been different,' he murmured.

'No, it . . .'

'Felicity, can you not see? I have lost my son—my only son.' As he looked up at her, she

228

could see that there were tears in his eyes.

'No, you haven't,' she insisted, moving closer to him. 'William is still your son. You are his father, and he loves you. You brought him away from London, so he would not destroy himself in a ruinous lifestyle, didn't you? He has not done that, has he?' Sensing that he was taking in what she was saying, she moved closer still and went on, 'He is an honourable man who has made a decision on principle, which is more than a lot of people ever do. I know that this is not what you had planned for him, but I think you should be proud of him.'

'Proud? You think I should be proud?' he said incredulously. 'You know the kind of life that I led before I took William away from London. Do you think I don't know that this is a judgement on me?' He closed his eyes, put out his hands towards her, drew a ragged breath and said, 'Oh, Felicity, help me!' Without a second thought, she put her hands into his and allowed him to pull her on to his knee. For a short time, they just held one another, she cradling his head against her breast, and stroking his hair in an effort to bring him comfort. Then they drew apart a little; their eyes met; their embrace changed as it had in the Sydney Gardens, and suddenly they were kissing one another again, each one as much the instigator as the receiver.

At last, after what seemed to be only

seconds, but could have been an eternity, they drew apart enough for James to whisper, 'Felicity—stay with me.'

'James, I can't,' she replied. 'You know that.' Even as she spoke the words, in her heart she was tempted to give way to him, even though she knew that it would be against all her principles.

'Please—just for tonight,' he added. Just for tonight! Was that all she was worth? The words acted like a shower of cold water, and they brought her to her senses. She looked round, as if suddenly aware of her surroundings, and scrambled off his knee.

'I must go,' she said, backing away. He remained in his chair, looking at her.

'Go on, then,' he said bitterly. 'Go and see who you can help next.' She was nearly out of the room. when he shouted at her, 'Whatever you do, don't give me what I really need!' She picked up her bonnet and cloak, then ran out of the house, not waiting for the footman to open the door for her. As she ran down the steps, she saw Christopher waiting on the pavement, standing next to a hackney carriage. She felt sure that the conflicting emotions to which she had been exposed over the past half-hour must be written all over her face, but luckily, her brother was so full of his own news that he did not take in her distress.

'The most amazing thing,' he said, after they were both seated inside. 'I have met Nick

Bonsor and he is coming to see you tomorrow morning.' These tidings were enough to take her mind temporarily off what had taken place between herself and James.

'Chris! That's marvellous! But how did this come about?'

Christopher laughed.

'I thought that would surprise you. After I left you, I decided to go back to Gunther's and see if I could get an ice. After all, they looked delicious, and our money is as good as anyone else's. When I got there, there was quite a crowd around the entrance, and all of them were so fashionably dressed that I felt like a country bumpkin all over again. They were talking and laughing, and I heard one of the gentlemen say, "Lord Nick has promised to buy us all ices!" Another one said, "I doubt if he can. All the Bonsors have their pockets to let." Then the third gentleman said, "After that slur on my family name, what can I say?" After he had spoken, he turned and saw me, and he could tell that I was taking an interest in what was happening. He strolled over to me and I quite thought that he was going to tell me not to listen to other people's conversations, or some such thing. But instead he said, "Is there any way in which I may serve you?" He was looking at me curiously, as if he recognized me, but we have never met.' Fliss smiled to herself. In some lights, there was a certain likeness between the twins and

231

Melissa, but none of them could ever see it.

'Go on,' she said.

'I told him who I was, and explained that you would like to have speech with him. He enquired where we were staying and said that he would be pleased to renew his acquaintance with you and that he would be there in the morning . . .' His voice tailed off, then he spoke again, anxiously this time. 'You haven't come to London in order to intrigue yourself with him, have you?' he asked her. 'Because I don't mind telling you that for all he was very civil, he looked very much like a loose fish!'

'Chris, do you really think that I would insist on my brother's accompanying me to London so that I might intrigue myself with a rake?' Christopher had the grace to look abashed, and admitted that it did not seem to be very likely.

'Did Sir James know where to find him?' he asked carelessly, but to Fliss's relief he was quickly distracted by the sight of someone falling off his horse, and when he next spoke, it was to speculate on what there might be for dinner, thus relieving Fliss of the necessity of answering at all.

*   *   *

That night in her room after she had prepared for bed, Fliss sat up once again with her arms around her knees, and remembered what had

232

taken place that day. She could still picture the way that James had looked. James, drunk in the middle of the day! She would never have thought that such a thing was possible, except that he had told her of his rakish past. The news of his son had hit him hard. Fliss tried to remember William, but it was quite difficult to get a clear picture in her mind. He had been at school, then university, and then he had gone on the Grand Tour. She vaguely remembered him being a polite, good-natured boy, somewhat like his father in appearance, but not so strongly built.

She went over in her mind the moment when, after they had kissed, James had said 'Felicity, stay with me'. Oh how she had been tempted! If he had not added those fatal words 'just for tonight' she might even have succumbed. He had needed her and she had rejected him, but he had only wanted her for one night, and she could not bear to belong to him on those terms. Every principle she had, and every canon of her upbringing shrieked against it. Besides, how could she possibly help Melissa if she were in the same position herself?

She sat for a long time, going over and over the scene in her mind, imagining how she might have responded better, or somehow directed things so that he could have realized that she cared, and so that he would have had no need to make that disgraceful suggestion.

Eventually, she stretched, and gave herself a little shake. It was no use thinking about it now. She could not change what had been said or done. Far better for her to get a good night's sleep, so that she would be fresh in order to confront Lord Nick in the morning.

The next day, after breakfast, Christopher asked Fliss if she would like him to be present, or at least on hand whilst she spoke to Lord Nick.

'For I don't mind telling you, Fliss, that as far as women are concerned I wouldn't trust him as far as I could throw him.'

'It's quite all right, Chris,' said Fliss reassuringly. 'You are absolutely right about him, of course, but I promise you that he has no designs upon me.' Her brother looked at her for a long moment, then nodded.

'I'll be off to have another look at St Paul's then, but I shan't go until he's arrived,' he said. 'It might be as well to remind him that you are not without a man to protect you.' Fliss smiled at him. He looked determined and dignified as only an eighteen-year-old boy can.

'Thank you,' she said warmly. 'I don't know what I would have done without you. Have you arranged for a private parlour for me when he comes?'

'Yes, I have, but I'm not sure that it's wise.' He gave her another long look.

'I promise you I'll scream if necessary,' she said, and with that he had to be satisfied.

Nick strolled into the inn at eleven o'clock, and bowed with his usual careless grace, a cynical smile on his lips. He looked a little thinner, a little paler, and a little more dissipated than when she had seen him last.

'Miss Wintershill,' he murmured with every evidence of pleasure. 'How delightful to see you once more. This is a happiness I had not anticipated.' Fliss had not known how she would feel when she met Nick again, but she was unprepared for the surge of anger that overwhelmed her as she came face to face with the seducer of her innocent sister. She would have liked to have slapped his smiling face there and then, but she had not come all the way to London to end the scene in such a way. Mastering her anger, she merely returned his greeting in a formal way, and said that she hoped he was well.

'Tolerably, ma'am. This is your charming brother, I believe, whom I had the pleasure of meeting yesterday outside Gunther's.'

'Certainly he is my brother,' replied Fliss. 'Whether or not he is charming is possibly a matter for debate!' Christopher grinned as they exchanged bows.

'And are any other members of your family here with you in town?' asked Lord Nick, taking out his snuff box and offering it to Chris, to that young man's great astonishment and gratification.

'No, there are just the two of us.'

'Indeed? And what brings you to London? Business or pleasure?'

'A little matter of business,' replied Fliss, looking at him deliberately. He returned her look with a blandly innocent one of his own.

'Indeed? Perhaps I may be of service to you, Miss Wintershill? London is full of sad rogues, I'm afraid.' He did not look in the least bit regretful, more impish, really, but Fliss was in no mood to respond to his foolery.

'Of that I am aware, my Lord,' she replied. 'My business is with you.' He looked genuinely surprised, then.

'With me? Ma'am, I am honoured, but I do not quite see . . .' His voice tailed off. Fliss turned to her brother.

'Chris, where is the private room which you have procured for me?' Lord Nick turned to her again with a smile, showing his teeth.

'My dear Miss Wintershill,' he purred under his breath, as they followed Chris to a small private parlour, 'you surprise me.'

'What do you want me to do?' asked Chris, looking very much like a ruffled terrier confronted with a large wolf, and very determined to defend his own no matter what the odds.

'Go to St Paul's as you planned,' said Fliss. 'His Lordship will do me no harm.' After one more long look at the disreputable nobleman, Christopher left the room and shut the door.

'You seem very sure of yourself—and of

me,' said Nick after he had gone.

'I am quite prepared to think the worst of you, my Lord,' said Fliss calmly, 'but I would have thought that seducing one sister from a family would have been enough, even for you.'

His smile faded.

'I see,' he said. 'May I respectfully suggest, ma'am, that you are talking about something of which you know very little?' He looked about him. 'Do you mind if I ring for some wine? I've a notion that I might need it.' Fliss signalled her consent, and a servant came almost immediately to take Lord Nick's order for a bottle of claret. They both sat down, Fliss sitting very upright in her chair, Lord Nick sprawling in his in a way that bordered on the insolent.

While they were waiting for the wine to be brought, Fliss said, 'What I do know, my Lord, is that a little while ago in Bath, a message was sent and no reply given.'

He was silent for a moment, then said, 'Perhaps the message merited no reply.' She was so astounded at this reaction, that, for a few moments, she was completely lost for words. At this point, the door opened to admit, not one of the inn servants, but the sturdy landlord, who put the tray down on the table, and said meaningly to Fliss before he left that if she were to require anything, he would be close by.

'You have some loyal defenders, ma'am,'

237

said Lord Nick as he poured. He offered Fliss a glass with a gesture but she shook her head.

'What do you mean, it did not merit a reply?' she asked, ignoring his last remark. He took a sip of wine.

'Precisely that,' he answered. 'Some messages need an answer; others do not.'

'But you could at least have come,' she cried, 'if only to say goodbye.' He sat looking at her, his glass in his hand. His expression was completely impassive.

'And why should I do that?'

Fliss closed her eyes for a moment, wondering what she could say to move this man, who was showing so clearly an utterly callous disregard for her sister's feelings. After a brief pause she opened her eyes, stood up and put out her hands to him.

'Lord Nick, do you not understand why I have come?' He had been looking down into his wine glass, still half full of the dark red liquid. Now he looked up at her and suddenly, it was as if he saw her for the first time. She had already risen. Now he did too. He took in her pallor, her distress, and above all the sombre nature of her clothing. All the colour drained completely from his face, and his glass fell from his hand unheeded and smashed on the floor, splashing the remaining wine across the polished wood boards like a pool of blood.

'You are in mourning,' he said hollowly. 'Oh God, Melissa . . .' No one hearing the anguish in his voice could have accused him of lack of feeling then. It took Fliss a moment or two to grasp what he must be thinking. When she realized, she hastily stepped forward and touched his arm.

'No! No, not Melissa! It was our mother who died! That was why we left Bath. Pray, Lord Nick, sit down and I will call for someone to clean this up.' He sat down in a chair by the table, and this relieved her, for he had been so pale that she had almost been afraid that he might faint. She poured some wine into the other glass and gave it to him, then went to the door to find a servant.

While the glass was being cleared away, Lord Nick sat at the table staring into the fireplace saying nothing, his glass in his hand. Before the servant left them again, Fliss asked for another glass. She had decided that she could do with something herself!

When they were alone once more, Lord Nick said, 'I didn't know about your mother. I'm sorry, but it doesn't change anything.'

'I see,' said Fliss, deciding to play her ace. 'Then I suppose there is no more to be said. Perhaps you could give me your direction before you go, then I can let you know.'

'Let me know what?'

'Whether you have a son or a daughter.'

He stared at her for a long moment, then at last he said, 'May I tell you, ma'am, that I do not envy James his married life if you are

239

accustomed to deliver body blows such as that in such swift succession? The poor fellow will be punch drunk before his honeymoon is over.'

'I am not going to marry James,' she said defensively, but was very conscious of the fact that her face was turning bright red.

'Really? Do you mind if I keep my own counsel on that one?' Fliss decided that it was time to return to the matter in hand.

'I notice that you do not ask if the child is yours,' she said.

'I don't need to,' he replied, getting up from his place at the table and walking to the window, where he stood with his back to her. 'I was the first with your sister, and she is not a light woman. There have been no other lovers—yet.'

'What do you mean—yet?' asked Fliss, coldly, after a long pause.

'She's a beautiful woman. Other men are bound to want her. She might possibly have had someone else in her eye, even before she gave me my *congé*.'

'I . . . I don't understand,' said Fliss, puzzled. 'What do you mean, she gave you your *congé*?'

'You know. In the message that we were talking about; the one she left for me with Ruth Stringer.'

Fliss shook her head in bewilderment. 'What message are we talking about now?' she asked him. 'I understood the message that she

240

gave said that she was leaving Bath because of our mother's death, but that she wanted to see you, and would you come to her.' She thought for a moment and went on, 'But you cannot have received that message because you did not know about Mama.'

'No, I didn't,' he said. 'Instead, I had a message telling me that we had had an agreeable frolic, but that she was now leaving Bath, and she did not want to see me again.'

'Lord Nick, you know my sister: does that sound like the kind of message she would send?'

'No, it doesn't,' he said quietly, looking down into his glass.

'Then why did you not come after her?' He said nothing. After a short silence, she added, 'There was something else, wasn't there?' He looked up at her then and smiled, a twisted smile with no humour in it.

'Acute of you. Yes, there was more to the message.' He sighed. 'She said that I was . . . too old. That's why I didn't come after her. Vanity, you see. She touched a vein of truth there. I am twice her age.'

'But Melissa would never, ever, have said such a thing,' exclaimed Fliss. 'How, then, could such a mistake . . .?' She thought for a moment. 'Ruth Stringer! Lissa always said that she thought Ruth did not like her, even while she was helping her to meet you, but I don't suppose she realized that Ruth would be so

241

actively malicious.'

'Ruth was more than malicious,' answered Nick impassively, pouring himself another glass of wine. 'After she had delivered Melissa's message, she hinted, rather less than delicately, that she might perhaps take up with me where Melissa had left off.'

'Oh no!' cried Fliss. 'What a perfectly dreadful girl!'

They were silent for a long time after that, then Nick said, 'Malicious or not, there was one thing the wretched girl may have got right: perhaps it would be as well to regard Melissa's and my liaison as an agreeable frolic, and no more.'

'Perhaps that is what it was to you, my Lord, but I don't think that my sister is in any position to look at it in that way,' replied Fliss a little tartly.

He coloured then, but replied in dispassionate tones, 'More fool her, then.' Fliss did not answer, because she could not think of the right words with which to defend her beloved sister, but she stood looking at him steadily until he went on, this time with more heat, 'Surely she must have known what manner of man I am.' His voice dropped again and he added, 'You must know it too. God knows why you've come.'

'I know what manner of man the world says you are,' ventured Fliss.

Lord Nick gave a derisive laugh. 'Oh, the

world is generally in the right of it. Believe me, she's much better off without me.'

'She's certainly much better off without someone in her life who is a rake and a wastrel,' answered Fliss.

'Then why have you come, if you believe that? Don't say that it was just to get money from me—which will be forthcoming, by the way—because you could easily have written to me to obtain that.'

'I have come because I believe that you don't have to be either of those things. There is no law that says you have to remain on this self-destructive course. The trouble is that so many people have been saying that you are a libertine and a care-for-naught for so long that you've come to believe that no other life is possible. Well, it is.' He had thrown himself back into his chair while she was speaking and now lounged as before in an attitude of studied insolence.

'Has it occurred to you, Miss Wintershill, that I like my rakish, self-destructive life? That I might not want to change?'

Fliss sighed. 'Lord Nick, I believe that there is little point in continuing this conversation for much longer. We have corrected some misunderstandings, and I am glad of that, and you have promised me money for the upkeep of your child. That, too, will be appreciated. However, I have just a few things that I wish to say to you before I bid you goodbye. The first is to tell you that my sister is in love with you, although I suspect that you know that already. I do not mean that she desires you as I believe many women do: she loves you—God knows why.

'The second is that Ruth Stringer was right in part. You are not old, but you are growing older. For how much longer will you be able to attract women? How long before they turn from you in disgust? How long before you are obliged to pay for female company? Already the marks of your way of life are showing on your face. Take a good look at yourself in the mirror, sir, and decide whether you like what you see.

'Thirdly, my sister is not enduring this pregnancy well. She is not eating enough or looking after herself as she should, and she is not in good spirits. Think how you felt when you saw me in mourning and thought that she had died. One day, a member of my family might bring you that very news, and how would you feel then?' She walked to the door and turned to look at him 'You have three things to think about, and now I shall give you one more: I shall do my level best to see that my sister survives this pregnancy, but she can best do that without any further distress. Therefore, my Lord, unless you come to her with words of love and a ring for her finger, I would ask you never to let her see your face again.' She opened the door and stood on the threshold. 'We return to Wintershill Court tomorrow. Goodbye, my Lord.' She left the room, closing the door behind her. She never found out how long he remained there motionless, sitting beside the table.

CHAPTER SEVENTEEN

After her interview with Lord Nick, Fliss went up to her room. She felt utterly drained, as if she had been busy all day. She went back over everything that she had said, and decided that although she might have phrased some things better, she had not left out anything of vital importance. Now it would be up to Nick to think about what she had said and decide how to act. She had to confess that she did not feel very optimistic. True, Nick had been very distressed when he had mistakenly thought that she had been in mourning for Melissa, but perhaps a man always felt like that about the death of a woman who had been his mistress. More significantly, he had made no avowal of love concerning Melissa, even though Fliss had told him how much her sister loved him. One thing was certain: the interview would have to remain a secret. If Nick was true to his word and made some financial contribution to support the baby, then Fliss might have to tell Melissa that she had seen him, but she would never disclose the nature of the whole interview.

She felt far more awkward about keeping the matter secret from Christopher after all he had done for her, but after a period of reflection, she decided that she had no alternative. During this visit, he had shown a resourcefulness that had impressed her, and a protective instinct towards herself that had surprised and touched her. If he discovered that Nick had seduced his sister, he might feel himself obliged to challenge the rakish nobleman to a duel, and Fliss knew from James's disclosures that Nick had killed his man at least once. She could not possibly expose Christopher to that risk, even if her lack of candour offended him.

He did display a certain amount of curiosity about Fliss's interview with Lord Nick, but accepted her explanation with an admirable degree of maturity.

'It's nothing to do with the fact that you are only eighteen,' she explained to him. 'Had it been anyone else in the world helping me, even Richard, or . . . or . . .' She hesitated.

'Sir James?' he put in a little mischievously.

'Yes, even Sir James,' she agreed with slightly heightened colour, 'I could not have disclosed the reason for my errand, for it is still not my secret.'

'All right,' he agreed after a moment or two's thought. 'But will you promise me something? That if it becomes possible to tell about it, I will be the first to know.'

'Yes of course,' she agreed, hugging him. 'My work in London is done now. Do you think you can arrange for us to return home tomorrow?'

As Fliss mounted the step of the mail coach on the following day, she looked round the inn yard, half hoping that Lord Nick might make an appearance. But the only person who came anywhere near, apart from the inn servants, was Mr Woodforde, who came out to wish them a pleasant journey. With a tiny inward sigh, she settled back against the squabs as the carriage drew out into the street. She felt another surge of anger as she thought about the man who had seduced her sister. But, even as she did so, she recalled the way in which Melissa had concealed her previous acquaintance with Nick, the lies she had told, and perhaps, most of all, the calculating expression on her face that Fliss had spotted from time to time. Of course, Melissa was her sister, and Fliss would always stand by her as she had promised, but maybe Melissa was not so innocent as she appeared at first, and perhaps she could be more of an equal match for Nick after all!

After an uneventful journey including a night's stay at Maidenhead, they found themselves safely back at Marlborough. Christopher had requested the landlord to have the family gig sent back to the Court, and this had been done, but there was a gig to be hired at the inn for a trifling amount, and this they used in order to make the last part of the journey home.

Christopher proved to be an entertaining travelling companion, giving her a lively account of the circumstances under which he was sent down, which seemed in some way to involve a pig dressed in petticoats, and let loose in the quadrangle of his college. Fliss was glad of his chatter, for it prevented her from dwelling on the two matters that were more or less constantly on her mind: namely, what would happen about Nick and Melissa, and what would happen between James and herself? In the dark watches of the night, it was much harder to keep control over her thoughts and, if she were honest, she would have had to confess that she did not sleep very much at Maidenhead. It would be easier, although possibly more painful, she told herself as she punched her pillow for the twentieth time, if she could know for certain where she stood on either of these issues.

Barbara had been so plausible in her mendacious explanations of Fliss's urgent need to go to Bath that her family greeted her return with an almost unflattering lack of curiosity. Only Melissa wanted more information concerning Mrs Salisbury's health, but Fliss's reassurance that she was not near so bad as had been thought at first was enough for her. Fliss looked at her anxiously. She was just as listless as she had been before the London visit. This was indeed something beyond her power to mend, although she tried all she could think of, from encouraging Cook to provide the most tempting fare possible within the family budget, to coaxing Melissa to take a little gentle exercise. Truth to tell, concern for Melissa at least enabled her to stop thinking about James during every waking moment. One bright morning, nearly a fortnight after her return, Fliss suggested that she might like to go for a walk, but as usual she shook her head.

'No, thank you,' she answered. 'I think I had rather stay in the house. Walking seems to tire me.'

'Then I shall go alone,' replied Fliss. She was just passing Christmas Cottage when she heard a voice calling her name, and saw that Mrs Grantham was waving to her from the front door. It was the first time that she had seen the fashionable widow since the evening of the Sydney Gardens expedition. She did not particularly want a conversation with Mrs Grantham, but she could not very well walk past and ignore her, so she opened the gate and went down the path.

'Mrs Grantham! I thought you were still in Bath,' she said.

'No, I left quite soon after yourselves,' she

said. 'Have you time to come in for a cup of tea? I have such a lot to tell you.' Fliss did not want to seem ungracious, so she accepted, even whilst wishing herself elsewhere. They went into Mrs Grantham's tiny sitting-room, and chatted on indifferent subjects until after the tea had been brought by Mrs Grantham's faithful maid.

'Dear Grace,' said Mrs Grantham when they both had their tea. 'She has settled here so well. I believe she will be as sorry to leave Christmas Cottage as I will be myself.'

'You are leaving Christmas Cottage? What a pity,' said Fliss dutifully.

'Yes, it is a shame, but I am sure that you will understand when I tell you the reason, which is that I am to be married.' Fliss was glad that she had put down her cup, otherwise she might easily have dropped it in her shock. As it was, she felt her heart sink like a stone in her chest. She knew what was expected of her, however, and although in her mind she was screaming against this latest blow that had been dealt her, years of self-discipline came to her rescue.

'Indeed!' she said. 'I am delighted for you, ma'am, and wish you very happy. I . . . I suppose I might guess who your . . . your husband is to be.'

'I suppose you might well,' agreed Mrs Grantham roguishly. 'After all, you had the opportunity of seeing us together in Bath. I must tell you that the attachment between us is of very long standing.' Fliss could not trust herself to say more, but tried to look interested. 'We first met in London, and were drawn to one another even then,' Mrs Grantham went on, 'but it was only when we met again recently that we realized to the full what we meant to each other.'

'How . . . how romantic,' Fliss managed to say. She picked up her cup in order to have another drink, because her mouth had become rather dry. She was pleased to notice that her hands did not shake. 'Is it known . . . that is, have you decided when the wedding is to be?'

'Quite soon, I think. After all, there is no reason for either of us to wait. I think we may travel to Italy after the wedding.' Italy! Fliss wondered whether perhaps this might mean a reconciliation between James and William. If so, then she could not help but be glad of it, even whilst it seemed as if her heart were breaking. 'When we return, I think we will probably live in London.' So at least they would not be living on the Wintershills' doorstep. Fliss thought of the house in Grosvenor Square. She had not seen very much of that house—only the downstairs room where James had been so drunk, and they had kissed. Better, though, not to think about that. The rest of the conversation was spent in exchanging commonplaces, and soon Fliss made an excuse to go.

'But you must come again before I leave,' said Mrs Grantham, as she walked with her visitor to the gate. 'I have so much enjoyed your friendship, and do hope that we will keep in touch.' Fliss promised to write, but resolved that she would not do so unless Mrs Grantham, or Lady Singleton as she would be then, wrote first.

Fliss found that she no longer wanted to visit Mrs Bonning as she had originally planned. What she really wanted to do was find some quiet place where she could cry undisturbed. She walked back towards the house, saying to herself all the time, 'I won't cry, not now. Not yet. I'm not going to cry yet.' She just about made it back to her room before her feelings overcame her strength of will, and when the door was mercifully closed behind her, she threw herself upon the bed and cried and cried until there were no more tears left in her. Never had she longed for her mother more than in that moment. Her mother had seen before anyone else, including herself, that James was the right man for her, and she would have immediately understood. Her father, still wrapped up in his own grief, would have no comfort to give, and Melissa had troubles enough of her own. No, Fliss would just have to bear this alone. At least if James and his new wife were living in London she would not have to risk being confronted every day with the happiness which she would give anything to be hers.

To take her mind off her own troubles, for about the millionth time, she went over the question of how Melissa's pregnancy could be managed. It could not be very far advanced so they had a little time before concealment would become impossible, but the squire would have to be told eventually. Had the pregnancy occurred sooner, it would, of course, have been possible to have passed the baby off as Mama's, but Fliss doubted whether Melissa would have coped well with that situation. It was, she knew, a deceit that was sometimes practised out of expediency, but she could not help regarding it with distaste.

The funds from Lord Nick were the key. Once they arrived, then hopefully there would be enough money for Melissa to establish herself on her own somewhere, not so far away that it would be impossible to visit her, but not so close that she would be known, for she would need to pass herself off as a widow.

Fliss managed to get through the rest of the day by concentrating on her various duties, and leaving herself without a moment to think. She was hoping that by the end of the day she would be so exhausted that she would fall asleep immediately. But sleep refused to come and when it did, it brought disturbing dreams. Finally, she woke at five from a dream in which she was pursuing Lord Nick in order to tell him something important but he would not turn round to listen. Then as she caught up with him, she realized that it was James, and that he had Mrs Grantham on his arm.

She knew that she would not sleep again, so she got up, washed and dressed. She looked critically at herself in the mirror. 'You look thirty-five if you look a day,' she told herself as she observed her white, tired looking face. It was ironic, really, that that morning, when she would have preferred everyone to ignore her, happened to be the one when her family became caring and solicitous. Her father looked at her at breakfast as if he had never seen her before.

'Fliss, my dear, you don't look well,' he said. 'Are you sure you aren't over-taxing yourself?'

Fliss smiled weakly. 'No more than usual, Papa,' she replied, hoping that that would be the end of the matter, but it wasn't.

'Then what is usual is too much,' he said mildly.

'Really, Papa,' exclaimed Fliss in a voice that was meant to sound amused, but came out instead as just rather wobbly.

'Fliss takes everyone's burdens on her shoulders,' put in Chris. This, or something very like it, had been what James had said in Bath. Before she could properly control herself, tears had come to her eyes and she choked on a sob. For a moment or two, the other three around the table sat in appalled silence. Then her father got to his feet, came round to her chair, and held her against him, patting her gently on the shoulder while she found her handkerchief. She had cried her cry out the previous day and these tears were of a mercifully short duration.

'I am so very sorry,' she said at last, putting away her handkerchief and trying to resume her normal tone. 'I cannot think what brought that on. Never mind, once I am busy . . .'

'You are certainly not going to be busy today,' said her father decisively. Everyone looked at him in surprise. They had not heard him speak in that tone since before their mother died. 'You have been working far too hard and you are going to rest. My dear, we all miss Margaret, and none more than myself, but she would never have forgiven me if I allowed you to turn yourself into a drudge.' He paused for a moment or two to collect himself, then went on, 'Barbara has proved herself to be very capable and she can manage what needs to be done for today, and Christopher can continue to pay penance for being sent down by helping me. So you see, we can very well manage without you and you can go back to bed and rest.' Barbara and Christopher both made assenting noises.

'Very well, if you all insist,' sighed Fliss, getting up from her place.

Barbara came round the table to give her a kiss and a hug. 'We do,' she said. 'And as soon as you are rested we will draw up a list of duties so that we can all help.' Fliss smiled and left the room. As she climbed the stairs she reflected how convenient it would be if the family could do without her completely. That would mean that she would be able to go and live with Melissa, certainly until the baby came and she was properly settled. Perversely, though, as she lay down on her bed, she could not help feeling a little resentment that her family seemed to be able to manage without her so easily.

She had gone upstairs without any expectation of sleeping at all, but when she woke she was amazed to discover that it was almost noon. None of her problems had vanished whilst she was asleep, but she felt rested and somehow better able to face them. Remembering that she had still failed to visit Mrs Bonning, she resolved to go and see her straight away. A walk in the fresh air would do her good, and if she did happen to walk round by a more circuitous route, thus avoiding the sight of either Roache Hall or of Christmas Cottage, then it was no one's business but hers.

She walked to the cupboard by the window and splashed her face with water from the ewer. She had just picked up a length of linen with which to dry herself when looking out of the window, she saw a horseman appear and realized that it was Richard. He glanced up at the window and waved, and on his face was a beaming smile. She hurried downstairs and reached the bottom just as Richard was coming in. He crossed the hall quickly and enveloped her in an enormous hug, so that she could hardly breathe.

'Richard?' she said questioningly as soon as she was able.

'Wish me happy, Fliss,' he said, and in his face there was not only happiness but deep content.

'Oh Richard, do you mean that Lady Susan has given her consent?'

'Yes, that's it. Come into the garden and I'll tell you all about it. The others must know straight away, and especially Papa, of course, but there are things I can tell you that I can't tell anyone else.' They went into the garden and by unspoken consent they ended up sitting once again beneath the statue of 'Old Redpath'. They were both quiet for a moment or two, remembering the last time when they had met there, under such different circumstances. Then Richard spoke. 'You remember that I left here to go to Bath?' Fliss nodded. 'I wanted to find out a little more about how Lady Susan had taken it that Alice was not to marry Paranforth after all. I thought that that might help me to think what I might do to help my suit prosper.'

'I don't suppose she was very pleased,' remarked Fliss.

'No, she wasn't apparently,' grinned Richard. 'Especially since most people didn't

257

realize, or didn't believe, that Paranforth and Mrs Grantham had known one another for years. Of course, when she was so insistent upon it, a lot of people began to think that she was starting a rumour just to save her face. Then the whole situation was made worse because Mrs Foreshore started droning on to Lady Susan in that way that she does, and Lady Susan cut her off by saying something rude. So Mrs Foreshore gave the rumour as much assistance as she could, with the result that half of Bath believed that Alice had been ousted in Paranforth's affections by a woman twice her age whom he had only just met. Fliss, are you listening?'

Fliss, who had turned pale at the mention of Mrs Grantham, started a little, and said, 'Yes, oh yes, of course! Richard, is it really true? I mean, that Mrs Grantham is to marry Mr Paranforth, and not . . . I mean, that is . . .' Her voice faded away.

Richard grinned. 'Of course it's true,' he replied, then added slyly, 'Why, who did you think she was going to marry?'

'I . . . I really don't know,' said Fliss, turning as red as she had been pale before.

'You can't possibly have been such a goose as to imagine that she would be marrying James, when everyone knows that he's besotted with you!'

'He isn't,' protested Fliss, putting her hands to her cheeks. 'Pray . . . pray don't be so absurd!'

'Say what you like, but I know what I know,' said Richard. 'Now, do you want to hear the rest of my story?'

'Oh yes, of course,' said Fliss quickly, not sure whether to be glad or sorry that this part of the conversation was over.

'Well, there was such a lot of gossip going around, that Lady Susan decided to return to town with Alice. I had already committed myself to meeting James in town, so you may guess how glad I was that I could fulfil my obligation and . . .'

'Do what you wanted to do anyway?' she suggested.

Richard grinned. 'That's right,' he agreed. 'Anyway, I travelled up to London and went straight to Grosvenor Square, but James wasn't there. He'd gone briefly out of town, apparently. So, to pass a little time—'

'Oh Richard, not gambling,' said Fliss reproachfully.

'Certainly not,' he replied with dignity. 'I've learned that lesson, I hope. But I did seek out Nick. My God, Fliss, if ever a man's ruinous lifestyle was written in a face, then it was spelled out clear in his. I found him at last in White's gaming for very high stakes and he looked fifty if he looked a day. He had a pile of money in front of him, but he looked indifferent to it. It worried me, Fliss, to see him like that. His game was just finished and he looked up and saw me. At once, a horrible look came into his eyes, as if he thought I were a ghost or something and he got to his feet, knocking over the table as he did so, and shouted at me, "Well? What have you come to tell me then? Answer me, damn you to hell!" Then I told him I was only looking him up whilst I was waiting for James and he sank down in his chair, with his face in his hands. It gave me a shock, I can tell you!' Fliss nodded. She could easily imagine what Nick had thought Richard had come to tell him.

'What did you do then?' she asked him.

'He was clearly in no case to go home on his own, so I collected up his winnings and helped him back to his lodging, where I stayed until James returned. I never saw Nick in that condition again, but although he was much as normal, I thought he looked rather preoccupied. In a day or two, James came back and I went to see him in Grosvenor Square. He also seemed as if he had a lot on his mind, but he certainly put forth his best efforts for me. He introduced me to some people in diplomatic circles, but the most useful person to me has been someone whom you have already met.'

He paused as if expecting her to guess, but Fliss simply said impatiently, 'Go on, Richard!'

'It's Paranforth! I told you that he and Mrs Grantham had known each other for years, didn't I? Apparently they were acquainted when his wife and her husband were still alive—although in a perfectly proper way, of course. Mr and Mrs Paranforth went to Italy, so that he could serve in the embassy in Rome. It was after his wife and Mr Grantham had died that they began to correspond. Anyway, he came to England only intending to stay for a short time, but he became ill and needed to go to Bath to recuperate, and that was where he and Mrs Grantham met again, face to face. They are to go to Italy soon so that he can take up his diplomatic post, and he has secured a position there for me! Just a minor one, of course, but one with many more prospects than the navy! You can imagine how thrilled I am.'

'Yes, of course,' said Fliss. 'But Richard, what about Papa? You can hardly arrange all this without any reference to him at all.'

'No, indeed,' he replied seriously. 'I am to speak to him this morning. James has promised to stand my friend if Papa does not understand, but I want to talk to him alone first.' He looked very dignified and grown up.

'Quite right, too,' agreed Fliss. 'But I am sure that he will be understanding. It is not as if you are intending to . . . to join a band of travelling players, or become a highwayman!'

'No, indeed,' answered Richard again. 'Well, I must not lose any time in speaking to Papa, then I'll tell the others. You can tell Lissa if you like. After all, she has already met

Alice and knows something of my hopes.' He grasped hold of both her hands and squeezed them. 'Oh Fliss, I'm so happy!' he exclaimed, then got up and hurried back to the house.

Fliss remained seated on the stone bench for a long time after he had gone. So James was not engaged to Amanda Grantham after all! Her heart should have been as light as air, and so it had been, the minute she had heard the news. When Richard had told her that he thought that James cared for her, she thought that she had nothing more to wish for. Then he had mentioned Melissa, and suddenly, for entirely different reasons, her chance of happiness with the man of her choice seemed as remote as ever.

The first reason for this was that she had promised Melissa that she would support her, and she would not break her word, no matter what the cost. The second was that the birth of Melissa's child out of wedlock would certainly be a cause for scandal if it became known publicly. Such a scandal, if it came to Lady Susan's ears, might jeopardize Richard and Alice's happiness. This problem could be solved if the matter were kept secret until after Richard and Alice had gone to Italy, but the dilemma as to what she could tell James still remained.

If he learned about Melissa's baby, then he might guess who the father was, and then what would happen? Would he feel obliged to challenge Nick to a duel? If he did, how would she live with herself if he were killed, or even if he were to kill his closest friend? Either way, she would be instrumental in either ruining or destroying his life. No, even if Richard were right about James's feelings for her, she could not let him guess the extent of hers for him. If he declared himself, she would just have to tell him that she did not want to see him again. However she looked at the situation, it seemed that there could be no happy ending for her.

CHAPTER EIGHTEEN

Fliss wandered up to her room to collect her bonnet. There was no sign of any of the children. She smiled wanly. Barbara was obviously ruling them with a rod of iron. She went back to the garden and picked a few flowers, then walked to the churchyard. As she passed Christmas Cottage, she could not help wondering when Mrs Grantham would go to join her fiancé. She sighed to herself as she reached the lych gate. The only fiancé that she had ever had and was ever likely to have was six feet beneath the soil.

She stood and looked at Rupert's headstone. He had been, if not precisely handsome, certainly well-looking, with a kindly, open face. Even while she thought of him, however, a picture of James came into her mind, and she knew beyond any doubt that those who said true love only ever came once in a lifetime were wrong. She had loved Rupert, but she now loved James with all her heart.

At that moment, she looked up and realized that James himself was watching her from a short distance away. Her heart thumped at the sight of him and she almost went to him. Then she remembered the huge gulf that Melissa's situation had placed between them and she knew that if he spoke to her of love, then for Melissa, for Richard and Alice, even for James himself, she had to drive him away. He took a step towards her.

'Felicity,' he said. 'I must speak with you.' She stood very still and waited for him to approach her. 'Felicity, I wanted to beg your pardon for my behaviour in London. I . . .'

'You mean, for the occasion when you were so drunk that you could barely stand,' she said coldly, her heart thumping even whilst she spoke.

'Yes, that was partly—'

'And for the way in which you suggested that I might spend the night with you?' she went on. He flushed.

'You do right to reproach me,' he replied in a mortified tone. 'In my condition, I was conscious only of my desperate need of you, and in no fit case to mind my words.'

'I think that the words you chose probably suited very well,' she said with heightened colour. 'No doubt any female off the street would have done!'

'No!' he exclaimed, horrified. 'No, you wrong me. You were the one I wanted; the one I needed. Felicity, I love you, I . . .' She had to cut him short before her resolution failed completely.

'Mama used to tell me what a gentleman you were,' she retorted. 'How wrong she was.'

'I may not have acted like a gentleman, but my professions are true. I do love you and I want to marry you. Please Felicity, listen to me!' He took a step closer but she took one back.

'Kindly keep your distance, sir,' she said haughtily. 'I cannot tell what you might do, and I have no wish to risk being mauled, as on that occasion!'

'Mauled!' he demanded, becoming so angry that he forgot to be tactful. 'I have no wish to offend you further, ma'am, but I would remind you that I was not the only one doing the mauling.'

'Oh how dare you!' she cried, excess of emotion lending her anger authenticity. 'Kindly refrain from approaching me again—upon any matter!' She turned to go, whereupon he took a step after her and caught hold of her shoulder.

'Felicity . . .' he said. She turned round at

once.

'And another thing, why do you keep calling me that? Everyone else calls me just Fliss!'

'Just Fliss!' he exclaimed, quite forgetting the need to be reasonable and conciliatory. 'Just Fliss! God in heaven, do you realize how furious it makes me when I hear you dismissed in such a way?' So saying, he seized hold of her, pulled her against him and kissed her hard. After a moment he released her, looking almost as shocked as she did. She stepped back and dealt him a ringing slap across the face. Then dropping the flowers which until then she had still been holding, she ran past him, back to the lych gate. He called after her, but she did not turn round. He stood for a moment in thought, mentally abusing himself for his crassness. Then he bent to pick up the flowers. He heard his name spoken, and looking up, he saw Mrs Bonning standing close by.

'Forgive me, Sir James, but I was on my way here when I witnessed part of your conversation with Fliss.'

'You mean, you saw how woefully I disgraced myself,' he answered, rising and handing her the flowers.

'Perhaps you weren't very wise,' she ventured. 'But I am sure that the situation is not irretrievable.'

'If you'll forgive me, ma'am, I must beg to disagree. But I must go after her, if only to

266

apologize—again.'

'I quite understand your wish to do so, but I am convinced that you will do so much better when you both have cool heads,' she replied. 'Come into the vicarage for a glass of wine before you follow her.' Seeing him hesitate, she went on, 'It will help you to regain your composure, and give her time to regain hers.' Recognizing the wisdom of her words, he turned and went inside, following her into the little parlour, where she rang the bell. The wine, when it came, was rather sweet for James's palate, but he sipped it and thanked her with grave courtesy. She smiled. 'You have beautiful manners, Sir James, but I fear that it is not to your taste. Please do not deny it, but permit me to send for something different.' This he would by no means allow her to do.

'There is nothing wrong with the wine,' he insisted. 'The fault lies in my inability to appreciate what is good.'

'I am very sure that that is not true,' she replied, looking steadily at him. They both knew that she was not just talking about the wine.

'Sometimes,' he went on looking down into his glass, 'one can fail to appreciate something until it is too late.'

'Yes, that is so, but I am sure that that is not the case in this situation.'

'You would not advise me to despair, then?' he said, looking up at her. 'Not even after what you saw?'

'Oh, I would never advise anyone to do that.' She was silent for a while. Then she went on, 'Sir James, you know that my son died six years ago. There have been times when I have been close to despair. Elias has been very good, but it has been painful for him, too, and there were occasions when we found it hard to help each other. If I had not had Fliss, I don't know what I would have done. But recently, I have started wondering whether her sympathy for my devotion to my son's memory has prevented her from finding happiness with someone else.' They were both silent for a moment.

'Mrs Bonning,' he said at last, 'I would never want you to betray a confidence, but has she ever spoken to you about . . . caring for someone?' The vicar's wife shook her head.

'She has not,' she answered. 'But I believe that there is someone for whom she cares very much. Sir James, I see that you have finished your wine and, much as I have enjoyed your company, I think that perhaps it is time you went after her.'

James put down his glass.

'Since we are speaking so frankly, ma'am, I feel bound to say that I do not see how she can change her opinion of me now.'

'I think that that is probably true,' she agreed. 'But I do not think that your idea of what she thinks of you agrees with mine.'

＊　　＊　　＊

When Fliss had run half the length of the village street she realized what a spectacle she was making of herself. She also discovered that James was not pursuing her. Not sure whether to be glad or sorry, she continued on her way home at a more decorous pace. After all, why are you being so foolish? she told herself severely. The worst is over. He has told you of his love and you have rejected him. All you have to do now is treat him with repulsive coldness whenever you see him, and he will soon fall out of love with you and look for someone else. It sounded simple, but the very thought brought tears to her eyes, which she dashed away impatiently.

She was still trying to reason with herself along these lines when she reached home, and saw that a gentleman was at that very moment handing over his horse to be led into the stables. As she drew nearer he turned round and she saw that it was Lord Nick Bonsor.

'Miss Wintershill,' he said, bowing over her hand. 'Good day.' She looked at his face. He looked if anything older than when she had last seen him, and she was reminded of what Richard had told her.

'Lord Nick,' she replied politely. 'I believe you have seen my brother.'

He smiled humourlessly. 'Your family

269

certainly has a strange ability to frighten the life out of me,' he replied. 'Yes, I saw him, and aged about ten years. Then I took your advice. I looked in the mirror, and I didn't like what I saw. May I speak to her?'

Fliss took a deep breath. 'Lord Nick, I believe I asked you never to approach my sister again, except under certain conditions. You remember what I said?'

He met her gaze squarely. 'Yes, I remember: "words of love, and a ring for her finger". I suppose you realize I'll make a diabolical husband?'

'I think that you can be any kind of husband you choose to be,' she answered.

'May I see Melissa?'

They looked at one another for a long moment, then she said at last, 'I'll take you into the house.'

'How is she?' he asked her as they walked together.

'Much the same,' she answered. 'No appetite, no energy, no interest in anything.'

'I'll have to see what I can do about that.'

Fliss took him into the house by a side door. Melissa she knew would be lying down on the day bed in the little drawing-room which faced on to the garden. It had no entrance from the hall, but could only be approached through the bookroom, so she knew that once she had taken Nick there, if she stayed in the bookroom then they would be left

270

undisturbed.

'Wait here,' she said to Nick, once they were inside the bookroom. He looked handsome and rakish as ever in his dark riding dress, but he seemed a little tense as well. Fliss suddenly caught something of what he must be feeling. He was on the point of confronting the girl whom he had seduced and then, as far as she was concerned, abandoned. Might he have come all this way just to be rejected? She prayed that by her interference she had not done them both a terrible disservice.

She went into the drawing-room. Melissa was lying on the day bed, a book in her hand, her gaze fixed on the view outside and her mind obviously miles away. 'Lissa,' Fliss said softly. Her sister looked round. 'Lissa, I have a visitor for you.' Fliss beckoned to Nick, and then stood to one side to let him come in. He waited on the threshold, looking at the girl on the day bed, so much paler and thinner than he had remembered. For a few moments, Melissa was very still, and he could not be certain of the nature of his welcome. He could not know that Melissa had dreamed of his coming so often and awakened to find that it was not real, that she was unwilling to trust the evidence of her own eyes. Encouraged a little by the fact that she had not actually turned away from him, he took a step forward and spoke her name. With that, her book fell unnoticed to the floor and she was on her feet, her face filled with colour, glowing and transfigured.

'Nick! Nick, my Nick!' she cried. He took two steps forward and caught her in his arms. Fliss looked at them for a long moment, before leaving the room and quietly closing the door behind her. She leaned against the door with her eyes shut. For a few moments, all she could think of was her dearly loved sister, and of how she seemed to have found happiness with the man of her choice, contrary to all expectations. Then suddenly, there came the recollection of how she had seen James, of how he had said that he loved her, and she had sent him away. With the advent of Nick, all barriers could be swept away; but what if James believed that she really was disgusted by him? What if he never came back? Suddenly she was filled with such a longing to see him and touch him that she wondered how she would ever be able to draw another breath.

Then, out of nowhere it seemed, she heard a voice very close to her saying, 'Felicity my dear, are you quite well? What is wrong?' She opened her eyes to see James bending over her solicitously. Because she had been thinking of him and wanting him so much, the sight of him operated so powerfully upon her that she forgot all about correct custom and form. So it was that instead of greeting him politely and assuring him that she was well and inviting him to have a glass of wine, and setting about a courteous explanation of her previous conduct, she simply put up her arms and pulled his head down and kissed him.

This was not the kind of greeting that Sir James had expected. He had parted from her in the churchyard, convinced that she was disgusted by his advances and wanted nothing more to do with him. The best that he had come hoping for was that she would forgive him and honour him again with her friendship. To say that he was surprised at her action therefore would definitely have been an understatement, but he was not a man to allow the grass to grow under his feet. With an alacrity only equalled by his enthusiasm, he put his arms around her, held her close, and kissed her back with a fervour equal to her own. Eventually they drew apart, and suddenly the enormity of what she had done dawned upon her. She blushed bright red, and would have fled the room.

James however, sensing her urge for flight, took hold of her firmly but gently by the arms and said, 'No, Felicity. Four times we have kissed, and three times you have run away from me. You're not going to do so again.'

She looked up into his face and put up a tentative hand to touch his cheek. 'James—I hurt you,' she said, and they both knew that she was not just talking about the way that she had slapped him. She moved away from him and this time he did not prevent her. 'The

273

things that I said—such dreadful things! You must have thought me mad!'

'No, I did not think you mad,' he replied cautiously. 'But you will forgive me if I tell you that I feel a little confused.'

'Oh I know, I know,' she said, shaking her head. 'I . . .' He took hold of her hands, which she had been wringing together, and led her to a sofa where they sat down.

'Listen,' he said, when they were settled, sitting decorously a foot apart. 'I think I know something of what you are feeling. I approached you at the wrong time and in entirely the wrong place.' He looked down at his clasped hands. 'Felicity, I know that you loved Rupert Bonning, and that he was young, upright . . . everything I'm not, in fact. I told myself that I could never come other than a poor second to him, but that I could at least be there when you needed me, to care for you and protect you, and that perhaps you would eventually come to look upon me as more than your father's friend. Thanks to my drunken behaviour and physical abuse of you, I even put that at risk.' Fliss reached out tentatively with her hand, drew it back, put it out again and rested it on top of his clasped hands.

'James, please—stop punishing yourself. Yes, I loved Rupert, but you have never come second best to him. Believe me when I tell you that you are the man I love, now and for always.' He looked up at her: their eyes met, then he pulled her into his arms and held her close.

'Then why did you send me away?' he asked her. 'Did I express myself so badly? Or . . .'

'No James, no. It wasn't your fault, I promise.'

'Then why?' She was silent for a moment.

'I can't tell you, I'm afraid,' she replied eventually. 'It's because it isn't my secret. Can you accept that?'

He smiled. 'I believe I can accept anything if you will kiss me again. Only this time, promise not to run away.'

'Never again, James,' she whispered against his mouth.

Much later, James said to her, 'Will you think me very arrogant if I say that there were times when I thought that you were becoming fond of me?' and here Fliss blushed, thinking of how she had kissed him in the Sydney Gardens—'but there seemed to be a barrier which I could not cross.'

'There were a number of people who suggested that you might be interested in Mrs Grantham,' confessed Fliss.

'And you believed them?'

'She is very attractive, and you obviously knew her well,' pointed out Fliss, very ready to concede that Mrs Grantham was the most beautiful woman on the face of the earth now that she knew that James was hers. 'And after all, every time I visited her, it seemed that you came to see her too.'

'My darling,' said James grinning, 'did it not occur to you that I might have another motive for visiting Christmas Cottage?'

Fliss looked puzzled for a moment, then blushed and said, 'Oh!'

'Oh, indeed! Whenever I came here, either I was collared by your father, or surrounded by the children when the only one that I really wanted to see was you. To track you down at Christmas Cottage seemed an obvious plan. Who told you that I was interested in Amanda?' he asked curiously.

'One of my informants was your aunt, so you see—'

'Elvira!' exclaimed James. 'I'll wring her neck when next I see her!'

'Oh no, pray do not, for she was so very kind to me and Melissa during our stay in Bath.'

'I'll take you back to Bath again soon,' promised James, taking hold of both her hands and kissing each finger in turn, in a way that she found disturbing and pleasant both at the same time. 'But this time, ma'am, I trust that I will not have to worry about whether you are attracted to Nick Bonsor, or any other man! I wonder if you realize how jealous you made me? Indeed, I became so incensed at one point that I had to come home. Well, it was either that, or murder Nick, or wring your neck, or all three!'

'Oh, was that why you returned to Roache

276

Hall? I was convinced that you came home to see Mrs Grantham.'

'No such thing; although I did see Amanda. As a matter of fact, it was she who encouraged me to return to Bath. She was convinced that you were not indifferent to me. The reason that I came away was to avoid seeing you flirting with a handsome rake.'

'There's only one handsome rake I want to flirt with,' said Fliss roguishly, which audacious comment, needless to say, meant that James had to kiss her again. 'Not but what you looked every inch the rake when I saw you in London—and please don't start punishing yourself again because of how you behaved on that occasion. Christopher was there and he looked after me well, and I think it did him a lot of good.'

'Come to think of it, you haven't told me yet why you were in London,' he said curiously.

She turned her head away. 'That's connected with what I was saying before. I can't tell you I'm afraid. Can you accept that as well? I realize that I'm asking a lot of you.'

'I believe so. Knowing you, I suspect that you were rescuing some member of your family from the consequences of their own folly.' She looked at him pleadingly. 'Very well, I'll say no more on that head,' said James. 'Instead, I want to tell you a little more about my reasons for being in that state, and what happened afterwards. I'd seen William, as I think I told you at the time, but that was not my only reason for going to London. I wanted to talk to a friend of mine in government circles, to try and discuss the possibility of a diplomatic post for Richard.'

'Richard has already told me. Oh James, is there no end to your kindness?' cried Fliss, hugging him.

'Let me get on with my tale,' he said firmly. 'I want to finish it so that I can pull you on to my knee, talk rubbish in your ear, and kiss you senseless.' Having no fault to find with this, Fliss held her peace and allowed him to go on. 'Having arranged things for Richard, I had my interview with William—you know with what result. I cannot recall ever being so angry before. I suppose it must have been that because I'd removed him from the London scene, I'd thought I'd made him safe; that the succession was secured. Then I found that with the decision he'd made, I'd lost him just as surely as Stephen had lost Tony. So, after shouting at him, and throwing him out of the house I proceeded to try to forget my sorrows by getting thoroughly drunk. That was when you came.'

'I'm sorry I ran away and failed to help you,' said Fliss regretfully.

'Oh but you did help me. Far, far more than you know. You gave me another perspective. You made me realize that William was entitled to choose another direction for his life, just as

I did, when he was ten years old. More than that, you made me realize that whatever he does, and wherever he goes, he is still my son. As soon as I was capable of rational thought or movement, I hastened down to Dover, but by ill luck, I just missed him. Crossing the Channel as soon as I could, I caught up with him in France, and you'll be glad to hear that I have made my peace with him. He has accepted my apology and has promised to write to me. I can't pretend that I'm happy about what he is doing, or that I really understand it, come to that, but I expect I'll come to terms with it.' Acceptance of his son's decision had not been easy for him, and no doubt he would still feel despondent at times, but the worst was over. Fliss smiled and squeezed his hand.

'You can visit him too,' she pointed out.

'So I can,' he agreed. 'Indeed, I have a notion to take you to Rome on our wedding tour. And now my darling, I have told you my story, and I am anxious to proceed with another matter.' He made as if to pull her on to his knee, but saw that a shadow had fallen across her face. 'What is it?' he asked her, sensing her distress but not knowing the cause.

'I have just realized: James, I am so very sorry, but I don't see how we can marry after all,' she murmured, looking down at her hands.

'Oh really?' he replied. He did not seem

noticeably dashed. 'And why is that, my love?'

'It's my family,' she said, distressed. 'How will they manage without me? Oh, I know that Barbara has coped very well in my absence, but that's a different thing to having to look after matters all the time. And Chris is away at university, and in any case, he doesn't want to care for the estate, he wants to design buildings, and as for all the others . . .' Her voice faded.

'My dear Felicity, for an intelligent woman, you do talk a lot of nonsense,' James replied firmly. 'It will be my privilege to care for your family. I intend to see to it that they have a housekeeper, a governess and a steward and that Christopher shall have the opportunity to follow his chosen profession. And don't forget that you will only be living a stone's throw from the end of the drive. And now that I have allayed your fears, my sweet . . .' He took hold of her hands.

'Are you sure, James?' she asked him anxiously. 'Just think of the expense.' Suddenly she thought of something else. 'Oh James, and the necklace! You paid for my necklace!'

'I believe I told you it could be a bride gift,' he smiled, 'although I have to admit that at the time I had not realized that I would be the lucky man!'

'Then why . . . ?' she began.

'Why did I buy it? It was on impulse, mainly. I really had gone in to buy something for a lady—a present for Elvira in fact—but after I had made my choice . . .'

'Well?' she prompted him.

'I have to confess that I couldn't endure the memory of your grief-stricken face,' he admitted, 'and from then onwards, I found myself thinking about you more and more. In any case, I cannot think of any way in which my money would be better spent!' He would certainly have pulled her on to his knee at that moment had not the door into the little sitting-room opened, to reveal Nick and Melissa standing on the threshold. Melissa's face was flushed most becomingly, and she looked better than she had done for some time, whilst on Lord Nick's countenance was an expression that James had never seen before.

'Nick?' exclaimed James, puzzled, as he rose to his feet. 'What the . . . ?'

'Good day, Sir James,' said Melissa.

'How wise of you to interrupt him, my love, before he said something unsuitable for our chaste ears,' drawled Nick, looking down at her. Then he took hold of Melissa's hand and, looking up at the baronet said, almost challengingly, 'Wish me happy, James.'

'My dear fellow, of course! With all my heart,' said James, clasping his friend warmly by the hand, whilst the two sisters embraced. 'But only if you will do the same for me.'

'At last!' exclaimed Lord Nick. 'I tried to give you enough hints, for anyone with eyes in his head could have seen that you were both in love weeks ago!'

'You are wiser than I, then,' answered James ruefully. 'My very best wishes to you too, Melissa, if I may call you that now! But how comes this about? Did you meet in Bath?'

'No, we met in London, two years ago,' said Melissa.

'There was a foolish misunderstanding which might have parted us for ever,' went on Nick. 'Thankfully, Miss Wintershill came to London to find me.' He smiled ruefully. 'She told me more home truths than I've heard in many a long year. Your Felicity is a remarkable woman, Solitaire.'

'I know it,' said the baronet smiling down at her and giving her hand a squeeze. Suddenly, Fliss knew that she did not have to explain anything more to James. He understood.

It was agreed that Nick should stay at Roache Hall with Sir James for the time being. Fliss invited them to come and have dinner that evening, after which they would both seek interviews with the squire. She walked with James to the bottom of the drive, leaving Nick to bid farewell to Melissa in the house. As they were walking arm in arm, very slowly so as to postpone the moment of parting for as long as possible, Fliss said thoughtfully, 'James—do you think they will be happy? I mean, in one sense I brought them together. I went to find Nick in London because I felt that he had a right to know about . . .' She stopped abruptly.

'Felicity, I know,' he interrupted. 'And before you say anything, I have guessed that their wedding will need to take place before ours. Nick's conduct . . .' He broke off.

'He did wrong, but Melissa did, too,' answered Fliss. 'At least they are together now. But even so, I feel a sense of responsibility.'

'Enough of that,' said James decidedly. 'You are not responsible for them. They are grown people and it is their life now.'

'But what if he does not make her happy? After all, he is a rake, and . . .'

'So was I, until I had powerful reasons for changing my way of life. Nick has a reason now, as well. No power on earth could have brought him here unless he had really made up his mind that this was what he wanted. I think that he wants to change, and that's half the battle.' They walked along in a deeply contented silence, until at last James spoke again. 'Felicity, there's one more thing I would like to know. When you ran from the house in London, I know you were shocked by my general behaviour—'

'Which was quite appalling,' Fliss put in in tones of strong disapproval.

'Which, as we both know, was quite appalling,' he agreed. 'But what was it exactly that made you run?'

'It was when you asked me to stay "just for one night",' she admitted. 'I didn't want to belong to you on those terms, James.'

'Yes, that was a mistake,' he replied. 'I want us to belong together for always.' He pulled her into his arms, and her response to his kisses left him in no doubt that his sentiments were entirely reciprocated.

We hope you have enjoyed this Large Print book. Other Chivers Press or Thorndike Press Large Print books are available at your library or directly from the publishers.

For more information about current and forthcoming titles, please call or write, without obligation, to:

Chivers Press Limited
Windsor Bridge Road
Bath BA2 3AX
England
Tel. (01225) 335336

OR

Thorndike Press
295 Kennedy Memorial Drive
Waterville
Maine 04901
USA

All our Large Print titles are designed for easy reading, and all our books are made to last.